"If you need a date to your sister's wedding, I'm available,"

Lucas said to Olivia.

"A date," Olivia murmured. "If that was all it was." She regarded him for a moment, then let out one long, resigned sigh. "My parents think that I'm…married."

"Married?" His eyes automatically dropped to her third finger on her left hand. "Are you?"

She shook her head. "Of course not. I thought if I could hire someone to be my husband, you know, just until after the wedding…."

It was the perfect opportunity to walk away, but for some reason he couldn't. The woman intrigued him, for reasons he didn't want to examine too closely, and so did her peculiar situation. She didn't strike him as the kind of woman looking for a knight in shining armor. "I'm still available."

"You mean it? You'll be my husband—at least for a little while?" Olivia asked.

He had to smile. "What is it the bridegroom says? I do."

Dear Reader,

Happy New Year to you, and Happy Birthday to us! This year marks the twentieth anniversary of Silhouette Books, and Silhouette Romance is where it all began. Ever since May 1980, Silhouette Romance—and Silhouette Books—has published the best in contemporary category romance fiction, written by the genre's finest authors. And the year's stellar lineups across all Silhouette series continue that tradition.

In Romance this month, bestselling author Stella Bagwell delivers an emotional VIRGIN BRIDES story in which childhood nemeses strike *The Bridal Bargain*. ROYALLY WED, Silhouette's exciting cross-line series, arrives with *The Princess's White Knight* by popular author Carla Cassidy. A rebellious princess, her bodyguard, a marriage of convenience—need I say more? Next month, check out Silhouette Desire's Anne Marie Winston's *The Pregnant Princess* to follow the continuing adventures of the Wyndham family.

Plain Jane Marries the Boss in Elizabeth Harbison's enchanting CINDERELLA BRIDES title. In Donna Clayton's *Adopted Dad*, a first-time father experiences the healing power of love. A small-town beautician becomes *Engaged to the Doctor* to protect her little girl in Robin Nicholas's latest charmer. And *Husband Wanted—Fast!* is a pregnant woman's need in Rebecca Daniels's sparkling Romance.

In coming months, look for special titles by longtime favorites Diana Palmer, Joan Hohl, Kasey Michaels, Dixie Browning, Phyllis Halldorson and Tracy Sinclair, as well as many newer, but just as loved authors. It's an exciting year for Silhouette Books, and we invite you to join the celebration!

Happy reading!

Mary-Theresa Hussey

Mary-Theresa Hussey
Senior Editor

Please address questions and book requests to:
Silhouette Reader Service
U.S.: 3010 Walden Ave., P.O. Box 1325, Buffalo, NY 14269
Canadian: P.O. Box 609, Fort Erie, Ont. L2A 5X3

HUSBAND WANTED—FAST!

Rebecca Daniels

Silhouette
R O M A N C E™
Published by Silhouette Books
America's Publisher of Contemporary Romance

TYVMFE!—and for making it better.
JAH, this one's for you.
Thank you for this,
that
AND the other thing.

 SILHOUETTE BOOKS

ISBN 0-373-19419-6

HUSBAND WANTED—FAST!

Copyright © 1999 by Anne Marie Fattarsi

This edition published by arrangement with Harlequin Books S.A.

Visit us at www.romance.net

Printed in U.S.A.

REBECCA DANIELS

will never forget the first time she read a Silhouette novel. "I was at my sister's house, sitting by the pool and trying without much success to get interested in the book I'd brought from home. Everything seemed to distract me—the dog, the kids, the seagulls. Finally my sister plucked the book from my hands, told me she was going to give me something I wouldn't be able to put down and handed me my first Silhouette novel. Guess what? She was right! For that lazy afternoon by her pool, I will forever be grateful." From that day on, Rebecca has been writing romance novels and loving every minute of it.

Born in the Midwest but raised in Southern California, she now resides in the scenic coastal community of Santa Barbara with her two sons. She loves early-morning walks along the beach, bicycling, hiking, an occasional round of golf and hearing from her fans. You can write to Rebecca in care of Silhouette Books, 300 East 42nd Street, New York, NY 10017.

Chapter One

"**C**onfidential Escort Service? Yes, I—I'm, uh, I'm interested in hiring a man."

Lucas McCall came to an abrupt halt outside the open door of Dr. Olivia Martin's office. Escort service? Could he have heard her right? Had she just said she wanted to *hire* a man?

The corridor outside the office was dark, lit only by what soft light escaped through the open doorway. It was late, almost ten, and the Mt. Rainier Women's Maternity Clinic was all but deserted with just a skeletal crew on duty. Still, Lucas glanced around self-consciously as he inched closer to the door. He was in charge of clinic security, not eavesdropping on its doctors.

"No, I don't have any particular preference. It really doesn't make any difference."

Her voice was low, and he had to strain to listen.

"No, no, you don't understand. I don't care what color hair he has."

She sounded impatient, frustrated and Lucas felt the air stall in his lungs. He glanced up and down the corridor again. Surely this wasn't what it sounded like. There had to be some other explanation—a joke, a dare, maybe some kind of research project? Why in the world would a woman like her need to hire a man?

"Look, you're not listening. All that doesn't matter. I just need someone for a few days—a week at the most. I'm willing to pay top dollar."

Lucas's boots moved soundlessly over the shiny linoleum floor as he inched closer to the door. He could hear the agitation in her voice, and was beginning to feel a little agitated himself. He was finding all this very difficult to swallow. Olivia Martin was willing to pay for companionship?

"No, no," she said with a heavy sigh, as though answering his silent question. "Believe me, that's not why I'm calling...I don't care if that's what everyone says at first...well, you're wrong, I'm *not* embarrassed, and I am not your sweetheart. Look, whether you believe me or not, I do *not* want to hire someone for...well, for *that*."

The air left Lucas's lungs in one long, silent breath. That. She didn't want to hire someone for *that*. Thank goodness.

"If you'd just stop talking for a moment and listen to me...yes, well, I don't doubt that you have heard it all before, sir, but the fact remains...no, I don't have a *thing* for blondes, I don't have a *thing* for any particular hair color, all I'm looking for is someone to be...well...to pretend to be..."

Her voice trailed off and for a moment he'd thought she might have hung up. Inching a few steps closer, he leaned forward just enough to take a peek around the corner. She was sitting at her desk, one hand holding the telephone, the other pinching at the bridge of her nose.

"Oh look," she said finally, giving her head a shake. "Forget it, forget I called...no, no...no, it doesn't matter...I've changed my mind."

She slammed the phone down with such force he jumped, ducking back and retreating several steps into the shadows. Feeling the cool surface of the concrete block wall against his back, he closed his eyes and drew in a deep breath. It had been a long time since he'd had a social life, but could things have changed that much? Was this how women met men these days, through an escort service?

It had been three years since the divorce, but ending his seven-year marriage had left a lasting impression. After Pam, he wasn't sure he would ever trust a woman again. He realized that all women weren't as manipulative or as devious as his ex-wife, he just wasn't sure he was able to tell which ones were and which ones were not. He'd *thought* Pam had loved him, he'd *thought* he could save her from a life without love and he'd *thought* she needed him, but what she'd been in love with, what she had needed, was his bank account.

It had taken him too long to admit what was happening, too long to see how she could use his love against him, how she could steer and maneuver to get what she wanted. He'd turned a blind eye to so much, tried to tell himself all he'd needed was to give her time, that she would realize marriage was more than wanting, or having and getting. But it had become painfully clear just how wrong he'd been on the day he'd found out about the baby.

She honestly hadn't been able to understand why he'd been so upset. Even though they'd never actually sat down and talked about starting a family, he just always assumed that someday they would. When he'd received a routine call from the doctor's office with a question on the billing for a procedure performed on his wife, he'd immediately been concerned. Pam had mentioned nothing to him and he'd never heard her complain about not feeling well. They'd been about to embark on a vacation around the world, a trip they'd both been looking forward to, and he wanted her to be up to the trip. He'd begun to wonder if she was keeping something from him, if maybe she wasn't feeling well enough to travel but didn't want to tell him for fear of disappointing him.

What a mistake that had been. He must have looked like a prize jerk rushing home full of worry and concern. When he'd told her about the call from the doctor's office she'd actually begun laughing as though it had been a joke—only the joke had been on him. She'd been preparing for their trip for months, shopping and putting her wardrobe together. Discovering she was pregnant had not only been unexpected, it had been an inconvenience. She hadn't wanted her figure ruined for the trip, hadn't wanted all those new clothes to go to waste.

At first he'd been too shocked to react. He'd known Pam could be self-centered and shortsighted but this was too much even for her. Defensive and unrepentant, she'd called him unreasonable when he'd gotten upset, telling him she'd only been thinking of them and their marriage. She'd seen the trip as a second honeymoon, time they needed together. The trip was special; they could have a baby any time.

Pam had left the next morning on the trip, but she'd left alone. He'd stayed behind to move out of their penthouse apartment and help his lawyers draft a divorce settlement she would accept. It had been useless to be angry with her. Pam had never pretended to be anything other than what she was—a vain, selfish woman. He'd been the one seeing things that just weren't there, the misguided knight so intent on saving the lady he'd forgot to look out for himself. But he would never make that mistake again. There were women in his life, but he kept them at an emotionally safe distance now. When it came to love, he didn't trust his judgment, didn't trust what he saw as being what was really there.

"Hello? Quality Escorts?"

Lucas's eyelids sprang open. Another escort service. Was the woman out of her mind?

Appearances certainly could be deceiving. He would have thought Olivia Martin would be the last woman who would need to pay for a man's company. Tall, slender, smart, beautiful—what man in his right mind wouldn't want to spend time with her? He'd been filling in for Gus on the night patrol for only a couple of weeks, and yet he'd spotted her the very first night. She was striking at a slender five foot nine and her long blond hair was always neatly secured in a tightly wound bun at the base of her neck. She wasn't arrogant or condescending like most doctors he knew. She had been cordial and friendly from the very first, stopping and exchanging pleasantries and engaging in light conversation. Meeting in the doctor's lounge had soon become a nightly routine, one he'd come to look forward to a little too much.

Lucas turned and looked at the open doorway. It had been a long time since he'd met a woman he actually liked talking to, a woman who was friendly and nice—and one who had no idea who he was. To Dr. Olivia Martin, he was just Luke, the security guard—a working Joe trying to make ends meet, yet that hadn't stopped her from being nice.

When Lucas McCall had left the Marine Corps fifteen years ago, the field of personal security had been in its infancy. But the need had been there and Lucas had not only identified it, he'd set out to meet it. What had made McCall Security different from all the other struggling businesses at that time was Lucas's willingness to tailor his service to the individual needs of his clients. From the mom-and-pop stores on the corner to high-rise corporate structures, from protecting the famous to guarding the infamous, Lucas designed and provided the kind of personal services needed. In less than a decade, McCall Security had grown to become the largest private-security business in Washington state, making Lucas McCall one of its most successful, and wealthiest residents.

Lucas pushed himself away from the wall. So what was he doing walking night patrol in a small medical clinic in the heart of Seattle?

He started slowly towards the open doorway. He knew that was a question a lot of the people in his own company would like to know, all those who thought it was a little crazy for the president and CEO of the biggest security company in the state to put on a khaki uniform and fill in for an absent employee from time to time. Of course he had his excuses down pat. He would tell those brazen enough to ask that he did it to "keep in the game," to keep sharp and on top of what was happening in the field, but that wasn't the real reason. He did it simply because he missed the old times, missed those early days when he'd been starting out, when McCall Security had just been him and a few loyal employees struggling to make a go of it.

And if he hadn't been filling in for Gus Jenkins, who was laid up with a broken ankle, he never would have met Olivia Martin, and wouldn't be standing there wondering what the heck she was doing calling an escort service.

"Yes, I was interested in getting information about hiring someone?"

Lucas heard her voice and rounded the corner, stepping over the threshold and into the lighted office. She was still sitting at her desk, but now a pencil in her free hand tapped nervously against the padded desk blotter, a telephone directory lying open on the desk in front of her. The wire-rimmed glasses she wore periodically were perched on her head, holding back the bangs from her forehead. It took her a few moments to realize he was there, but when she did, the pencil stopped in mid-tap.

"Uh, I, uh…" Spotting him, she sat up, then caught the pencil against the edge of the desk and snapped it in half. "N-never mind," she said into the telephone, dropping it back into the cradle. She looked up at him and smiled nervously. "Luke, h-hello. I didn't see you standing there."

"Am I interrupting something?"

Her gaze dropped to the telephone. "Oh that, I was just…" She glanced back, giving her head a shake, while making a dismissing gesture with her hand. "That was…nothing." She laughed nervously again. "Did, uh, did you need to see me about something?"

"No," he said simply, shaking his head. "Just doing my rounds and saw your light. Everything all right in here?"

"In here, oh sure, yes, everything's fine," she insisted, coming quickly to her feet. "I was just…" She shot another nervous look at the telephone and swallowed hard. "I was just making a few phone calls."

"I heard."

Her gaze shot back up at him. "Y-you did?"

"Yes, I did."

"Then you're probably wondering…" She tossed the broken pieces of pencil on to the desk. "I mean, that must have sounded a little strange…"

"Look, it's really none of my business," he said, cutting her off.

"But I know it sounded like I was calling an…an…" She cleared her throat loudly, struggling.

"An escort service," he said, finishing for her.

"Yes, an escort service," she murmured, taking a deep breath. "But I really wasn't...I mean I was— calling that is, but not for...well, you know, not for...for..."

"For *that*."

She stopped, giving him a helpless look. "Oh, Luke, I'm in trouble."

He didn't miss a beat, didn't stop to think, didn't even see it coming. Before he knew what hit him, his mouth was open and the words were out. "Anything I can do to help?"

Olivia wished a hole would open up beneath her and swallow her whole. She couldn't remember having been so embarrassed, but then she'd never been in a situation like this before either. What must he think? She must have been out of her mind to call those crazy places. It was just that she'd been so desperate, and there had been no one to turn to for help.

"You're sweet to ask," she said with a heavy sigh. "But I'm afraid not." She turned and gestured to the telephone, pointing as though she was identifying it as the guilty party in a crime. "And I'm sure all that on the phone just now must have sounded pretty strange."

"You calling an escort service?" He shrugged one shoulder. "Maybe a little."

There was something so endearing in his lopsided smile, something so charming and honest that it made her forget about feeling awkward and embarrassed.

"Oh, brother, I really must be losing it," she sighed, laughing. "But it seemed like such a good idea at the time."

"Hiring an escort sounded like a good idea to you?" He laughed too. "Now I really *am* intrigued."

She liked the sound of his laughter. "Well, if you need to hire a man, where else do you go?"

"Do you need to hire a man?"

"Just for a little while." It was only then that she glanced up and saw his confused expression and realized how that must have sounded to him. "Oh! No." She shook her head emphatically, getting embarrassed again. "No, no, not for…well, you know, not for…"

"For *that*," he said quietly.

There it was again. That sweet, captivating smile of his that was both soulful and full of humor, and she felt herself relaxing again.

"Right, not for that." She laughed again, taking a deep breath. "This keeps getting so confusing."

"It is a little unusual."

"I suppose," she admitted. "But don't escort services have people who are just…you know, just…"

"Escorts?"

"Exactly!"

"I have to admit I wouldn't know much about that," he confessed. "I kind of think there are escorts and then there are…*escorts*." He arched a brow. "I guess it all depends on what kind you're looking for."

"Well certainly not *that* kind." She reached down

and flipped the telephone directory closed. "I just needed someone to go somewhere with me."

"To escort you."

"Right," she said, hearing defensiveness in her voice despite her best efforts to stop it. It all sounded so ridiculous now. "Is that so unusual?"

"Well, actually," he said slowly, watching as she sat back down. "I think it is."

"I know," she sighed heavily, sinking back. "You're right. I just didn't know what else to do."

"You need someone to take you somewhere?" he asked after a moment.

She nodded. "My sister's wedding."

"You can't just go by yourself?"

She groaned loudly. "Absolutely not."

"You don't have a friend you could ask—one of the other doctors maybe?"

She shook her head. "You don't understand, it's not that simple. My sister's wedding…it's in California…in Santa Barbara."

"So what's that?" he insisted, making a careless gesture with his hand. "An hour by plane? Two maybe? That's not so much to ask."

Not much to ask. Olivia felt a dull throbbing at her temples. If he only knew. "It's more complicated than that."

"You need a date for your sister's wedding, sounds pretty simple to me."

"A date," she murmured, leaning forward and resting her elbows on the desk. "If that was all it was." She looked up, regarding him for a moment. "You know, you're awfully sweet to be listening to all this."

"I don't know about that, but I have to admit, you've got me curious. I mean, if you just need someone to go to your sister's wedding with you, I'm available."

Lucas was sure there had been some kind of mistake. Those words couldn't possibly have come from him—it was impossible. He didn't say things like that anymore, didn't go leaping to the aid of damsels in distress. He'd given all that up after Pam, had steered clear of women who would look at him with soft, vulnerable eyes. He didn't fall for those typically feminine ploys and gimmicks any longer. He was simply too smart and too jaded to let some woman make him act like a misguided knight ready to save her.

"You know," she murmured, sitting up slowly. Her dark eyes narrowed, examining him. "That's not a bad idea." She slowly rose to her feet. "You wouldn't mind?"

Lucas swallowed. "I, uh, I offered, didn't I?"

"It means several days though, maybe a week," she pointed out. "Would getting the time off be a problem?"

He relaxed. She'd just handed him the perfect excuse to back out, a chance to gracefully withdraw his offer. After all, to her he was just another working guy living paycheck to paycheck. All he had to do was tell her he couldn't afford to take the time off. That was all he had to do.

"I've got some time coming. It shouldn't be a problem."

The words floated out of his mouth and hovered

in the air above his head. An eerie peace descended upon him, the peace a condemned man feels on the morning of his execution, the peace of knowing what is to come, what was inevitable. And he knew what was inevitable—it was inevitable that he would never learn his lesson, that he couldn't seem to resist wanting to be the hero, wanting to save a maiden in trouble. Somehow, someway he'd managed to do it again, he'd jumped in with his eyes wide open and he had no one but himself to blame. He just prayed she'd have more sense, that she'd laugh off his offer and politely turn him down.

"Of course I'll take care of all the expenses," she said, her enthusiasm building. "And I'll certainly compensate you for your time."

He shook his head, barely able to hear her for the ringing in his ears. "That won't be necessary."

"No, no," she said adamantly, quickly rounding the desk. "I insist. I really do." She stopped when she reached him. "But before you say anything more, there is one other thing."

"Okay," he said cautiously.

She took a deep breath. "I know this is going to sound screwy."

"Screwy," he repeated. "You mean screwier than the escort service?"

She nodded. "A lot screwier." She stopped and released a breath in one long resigned sigh. "My parents think that I'm...married."

The ringing in his ears abruptly stopped. "Married?"

"Married."

His eyes automatically dropped to the third finger

of her left hand. Was it possible after spending as much time with her as he had that he hadn't noticed? "Are you?"

"Of course not." She followed the line of his gaze and rubbed her bare finger self-consciously. "If I was married I wouldn't be in this mess."

He shook his head, confused. "Oh boy, Doc, I'm afraid you're losing me again."

She looked up at him and winced. "I told you it was complicated."

Her expression was so cute and reflected the absurdity of it all that he couldn't help but laugh. "Okay, now let me get this straight. You need someone to go to your sister's wedding with you because you can't go alone and you can't go alone because you told your parents you were married, but you're not—married, that is." He gave his head another shake. "Have I missed anything?"

"No, no. You've got it, that's right," she assured him, excitement returning to her voice. "And I thought if I could hire someone, you know, just until after the wedding..." She paused for a moment, shrugging. "It seemed so simple at first."

"So you don't really need someone to be your date."

She shook her head. "No."

"You need someone to be your husband."

She nodded. "Right."

He considered this for a moment, then looked at her and nodded. "You're right, it is complicated."

She picked up her purse, slipping the long strap over her shoulder. "I'll understand if you want to withdraw your offer."

Lucas followed her out of the office and into the corridor. There it was again—another perfect opportunity to turn around and walk away, but for some reason he couldn't. The woman got to him, for reasons he didn't want to examine too closely, and so did her peculiar situation. She didn't strike him as the kind of woman looking for a knight in shining armor. She just needed someone to help her out, to do her a favor. Doing a friend a favor wasn't a bad thing, he rationalized in his head, and that was really all he'd be doing. The situation was unique, to say the least, didn't he at least owe it to himself to satisfy his own curiosity?

He flipped the switch, turning out the lights, and pulled the office door closed as they started down the corridor together. "No, the offer still stands."

"You mean it?" she asked, stopping as they reached the double doors leading to the clinic's parking lot. "You'll be my husband—at least for a little while?"

He had to smile, reaching around her to pull one of the heavy doors open. "What is it the bridegroom says? I will."

Olivia slipped the key into the ignition and turned to watch Luke walk back across the parking lot. She really must be out of her mind. The man had to think she was crazy and who was she to argue. What she was asking him to do was crazy. Still, in less than a week she would introduce him to her entire family as her husband. How was she ever going to pull it off?

She paused for a moment, closing her eyes and

envisioning a picture in her head. They were all standing there together—her mother, her father, herself and Luke. *Hi, Mom, Dad. This is him, this is my husband. This is Luke. Luke—*

Her eyes sprang open. Luke what? Luke *what?* She'd just asked the man to be her husband and she didn't even know his last name!

Was it any surprise there was no one special in her life? She just didn't know how to go about the dating ritual anymore—not that she'd actually *dated* Luke. Besides, given the circumstances, she was hardly a candidate for dating at this point. Still, she had been meeting him in the doctor's lounge almost every evening for the last couple of weeks and while they'd talked about nearly everything under the sun—politics, literature, sports, religion—last names just never seemed to come up in the conversation.

She groaned, leaning forward and rapping her forehead against the steering wheel. She had to keep in mind why she was doing this, had to remember the promise she had made and the obligation she had accepted.

Rachel and Ted Evans were her oldest and dearest friends and when they had come to her to ask a very special favor, she'd listened with interest. As a doctor, she understood all the technical jargon and medical lingo used to describe the condition that made it impossible for Rachel to carry a child to term, and as a woman she understood just how heartbreaking it had been for her friend to know she could never have a child of her own. Rachel and Ted wanted desperately to have a family and she couldn't have imagined two people more deserving and two who would have made better parents. So when they asked if she would consider having their fertilized egg implanted in her womb and have her carry their child for them for the next nine months, she had agreed. It had not only seemed like a practical solution to their problem, but a small sacrifice to make if it meant giving two wonderful people the family they deserved.

Still, there had been obstacles to overcome, in spite of how willing she'd been. Joshua Hille, Rachel's doctor, was a stickler for detail and as a woman who had never before been pregnant, Olivia hadn't fit within the guidelines as an acceptable surrogate. His concerns that she might bond too strongly with the child had been valid, but after several sessions together, and given her professional expertise in the field, Olivia had been able to convince him she would be able to remain objective.

Olivia opened her eyes and sat up, remembering that day nearly four months ago in Dr. Hille's office when he'd finally given them his okay. They'd all cried. Ted and Rachel were thrilled to have a chance at a family, and selfishly she found herself welcoming the opportunity to experience what she'd seen and assisted in hundreds of times before—pregnancy and childbirth.

Twisting the key in the ignition, the engine of her aging car roared to life. It had been almost three months to the day since she'd gotten word from the lab that the procedure had worked and that she was carrying a child. She had been so excited, and knew Rachel and Ted would be excited too. She must have called their number a dozen or more times during that afternoon, leaving message after message on the answering machine. She'd nearly gone crazy waiting for them to call her back, but when hour after hour passed and her telephone remained ominously quiet, she'd known instinctively that something was wrong.

The accident had been terrible. The official from the coroner's office had told her something about a drunk driver and a pickup truck jumping the center divider, but not much had sunk in. All she remembered hearing when the call had come in to her office the next morning was that Rachel and Ted were gone, killed instantly in a fiery crash that had ended their hopes and their dreams just as it had ended their lives.

Olivia slipped the car into gear and slowly backed out of her parking stall, emotion feeling thick in her throat. It had been almost too horrible to comprehend, too senseless to conceive that such an awful thing could have happened, that Rachel and Ted were gone and had died never knowing their child was alive and growing inside of her.

As she guided the car back, the headlights caught Luke's tall frame, his tan khaki uniform looking almost white in the light. If Mr. Whatever-his-last-name-was thought he had been confused before, what would he do if he knew the entire story? At three months, she still showed no outwards sign of her condition, but that would change before too long. Would he still want to meet her then? Would he still look at her the same way, the way that made her think about him long after she'd left the clinic?

She eased her foot down on the brake, stopping

just long enough to shift the car into drive. It had been a long time since she'd worried about making explanations or excuses to her parents, but this had been different. If Rachel and Ted had lived, no one would have ever had to know about the special favor, but all that had changed. With Rachel's parents gone, and Ted's widowed mother in a rest home, their baby had become her baby, a child she would raise as her own. It wasn't as though her parents wouldn't understand, they were wonderful people and would support her in anything she wanted to do. They were going to make wonderful grandparents, she just didn't want the unconventional manner in which the baby was conceived to interfere or inhibit how they would feel or interact with the child.

She watched as Luke stopped at the steps leading back to the clinic. Reaching for the flashlight on his belt, he flipped the switch, sending a shaft of light into a dark corner of the lot. A security guard probably encountered a lot of unusual things on the job, but they probably didn't get proposed to on the job very often.

"Oh, Olivia," she mumbled into the silence of the car. "What in the world are you doing?"

The idea had started out simple enough and yet had seemed so perfect. It wasn't as though she had started out wanting to be dishonest. As a matter of fact, she found being in the position of someone who is less than truthful to be very uncomfortable, but it seemed unavoidable. Her intentions were good, her motives pure and she honestly believed she was doing what was best for everyone. She may have shocked her parents when she'd called them

last month with news that she had "eloped," but
they'd also been delighted. It had been her idea to
follow her convenient marriage with a just as convenient divorce that would happen sometime in the
very near future. She hadn't told them yet about the
baby, wanting to give them a little time to digest the
news of her marriage before hitting them with another bombshell. With them believing her married,
the pregnancy could then be easily explained and
her phantom husband could have been out of the
picture and long gone before anyone ever had a
chance to meet him.

Flipping the flashlight off, Luke lifted a hand to
wave to her as she turned the car to pass and she
felt a sudden tightness in her chest. What her plan
hadn't accounted for was her younger sister suddenly deciding to get married as well.

She'd very nearly panicked when Monica had
called to tell her about the wedding and to ask her
to be matron of honor. Immediately her mind had
begun scrambling for an excuse she could use, some
reason she could give to gracefully decline Monica's
request and avoid having to attend. Only Monica
had sounded so happy and so excited, Olivia realized she not only felt obligated to go, she wanted
to. The only problem was she suddenly had to pro-
duce this new husband of hers—and fast!

Waving as she passed, Olivia felt the tension in
her chest turn heavy. She had a husband now, even
if she didn't know his name. She just hoped she
knew what she was doing.

Chapter Two

"That's Aunt Anne, right?"

"No, no, no," Olivia said, bending down and shoving her canvas bag under the seat in front of her. "That's Aunt Kathleen. Aunt Anne has Chris and Kristin. It's her husband, my Uncle Jake, who wears the cowboy hat all the time—only we never call her Aunt Anne, we call her Poo Paw."

"Poo Paw?"

"Right, but you don't have to worry about them for a while because they'll probably not arrive until a day or two before the wedding."

Lucas pressed up against the seat, letting another passenger squeeze past him in the aisle. He'd had seven days to try and get this all straight but obviously that hadn't been long enough. Chris, Kristin, Poo Paw, Papa—he was more confused than ever. He may only be playacting at being a husband, but there was nothing make-believe about the family he was about to meet.

"Now, let's go over this again," Olivia instructed, straightening up. "Aunt Kathleen is married to Maury. He's a dry cleaner and they live in Redlands. They have the twins boys, Kevin and Joseph, and it was their daughter Robyn who was going to marry the doctor. My mom and Aunt Kathleen love each other to bits but there's always been this rivalry thing between them and Aunt Kathleen really wanted a doctor in her family too—we talked about that, remember?"

"Uh, I'm not sure."

"Anyway Robyn left the doctor at the altar and eloped with the gardener they'd hired to do their backyard for the wedding. Is this sounding familiar?"

"Oh, wait—the gardener! Now I remember," he said, nodding, names spinning around in his head like leaves caught in a dust devil. "His name is...is..."

"Sam."

"Right, Sam. Good old Sam. Sam the gardener. They live in Santa Barbara now, right?"

"Right."

"Okay, I got it now," he said, nodding again. He deposited his carry-on bag in the overhead compartment above his seat. "So does the family call him Sam, or do you like calling him something else? Poo Poo? Poe Poe? Pee Pee?"

"No, we just call him Sam," Olivia answered dryly, but she couldn't help smiling. "But just be warned, even though Sam is a terrific guy and he and Robyn are very happy..." Her smile broadened to a full grin as she pushed a long strand of hair behind her shoulder. "Aunt Kathleen's still a little sensitive on the subject. Think you can remember that?" She paused for a moment. "Luke?"

"Hmm...what?" He jumped, giving his head a shake. He'd been staring right at her, but he couldn't seem to remember what she'd been saying. A beam of sunlight had come streaking through the small window of the airplane, distracting him as it played through her hair, turning it white-gold.

His mind had suddenly flashed a vision in his brain, a vision of those long, silky strands trailing over his bare chest feeling warm and soft and delicately scented.

"You okay? You looked like you were a million miles away."

"I'm sorry," he apologized, shaking his head again. "I got thinking about something else."

"Well, this can't be very interesting," she admitted honestly. "I've had my whole life to get this straight, you've had only one week. It must be pretty boring."

"No, no," he insisted, feeling foolish now. "I think I'm getting it. Keep a lid on the gardening talk—except with your mother. She raises roses, right?"

"Orchids."

"Orchids, right, I remember now." He slid into the narrow seat beside her, adjusting his weight in an effort to make his long legs fit into the narrow space. "Now Aunt Kathleen. She's the one you call Aunt Kate, right?"

"No, no. Aunt Kate is my *father's* sister," Olivia explained, buckling the seat belt together across her lap and pulling it snug. "Aunt Kate never had any children of her own, just a stepdaughter Sherry. When she was about eleven or twelve, Sherry's mother met and married some man who lived in Maryland or Maine, I forget. Anyway, Sherry didn't want to move so she went to live with Aunt Kate and Uncle Patrick and when Uncle Patrick died a couple of years later, she stayed on with Aunt Kate."

"They must have been close for her to have wanted to stay with her stepmother instead of moving back with her mother."

Olivia shrugged carelessly. "I think it might have had more to do with Sherry's mother not being too anxious about having her back. Anyway, Sherry's a social director for one of those cruise lines now."

"Really? Must be interesting."

"Oh, I'm sure it's just a thrill a minute," Olivia muttered dryly. "I'm just grateful she's out on the high seas somewhere and won't be at the wedding."

The open sarcasm in her voice had him turning to her. "Oh?"

"There's a little history between my cousin Sherry and myself," she confessed with a small sneer.

"So it would seem."

"Sherry and me...well, let's just say she's not exactly one of my favorite people."

"No?"

"No, and I'm sure I'm not one of hers either."

Lucas settled back in his seat, mulling over this

new information. It was obvious from the way Olivia spoke of her family that she held them in high regard. Discovering there was one that she didn't made him curious.

"Interesting," he said. "So you two don't get along so well, I take it."

"Let's just say we never...clicked."

"Clicked."

"But we won't go there," she advised. "Just believe me, if she were to be at that wedding, neither one of us would get much rest. She'd be asking questions, making comments, poking, prodding..." She stopped and shook her head, sighing heavily. "I'm *really* happy she's not going to be there."

"When you put it that way," he said, turning his head against the seat to look at her, "I'm sort of happy myself."

"But, we can relax," she said with a satisfied sigh. "My mother has assured me she is somewhere in the Caribbean as we speak judging Macarena contests and organizing shuffleboard tournaments so we don't have to worry. And my Aunt Kate is really nice—honestly. You're going to love her—and her name happens to be Kathleen too."

Lucas got the distinct impression there was more to this strain between Olivia and her cousin than she was saying and he had to admit to being curious about it. But it was obvious Olivia didn't want to talk about it and it really wasn't any of his business.

"I'm never going to remember all this, you realize that don't you?" he said, lifting one end of the seat belt and searching for the other.

"I know," she said in an understanding voice.

"And I know it sounds pretty screwball—it *is* pretty screwball—but you'll do fine." She reached up and adjusted the small air vent on the panel above her seat. "Just talk golf with my father and compliment my mother on her orchids and they'll love you."

"Golf I can handle," he assured her, having been termed a bit of a golf nut himself. "And orchids I can handle. It's not talking about weddings and gardening with Aunt Kate that I'm worried about..." He stopped and shook his head. "I mean, Aunt Kathleen." He gave his head another shake. "I know it's not Poo Pee."

"Poo Paw."

"Whatever." He snapped the two ends of his seat belt together. "Maybe I just shouldn't talk at all, how's that?"

"It's a thought," she acknowledged, nodding. "Then of course, there's always the weather. Can't get into too much trouble talking about the weather."

"The weather," he mumbled, settling back against the seat and closing his eyes. "I'll have to remember that."

The gentle vibration of the plane as it taxied down the runway almost felt soothing, even though he felt anything but relaxed. In the seven days since he'd agreed to play Olivia Martin's husband, he'd been barraged with a wealth of information. Of course he'd dutifully memorized the cover story she'd concocted on how they met and married, but he had also learned a whole lot more. He may not have known the woman long, but she was hardly a stranger to him any longer.

Still, when he'd met her at the airport this morning, he'd barely recognized her. It was the first time he had seen her outside the clinic and the change in her was dramatic. Without the wire-rimmed glasses and the tightly wound bun at the base of her neck, she'd practically looked like a different person. Her eyes looked softer and darker without the glasses and her hair was much longer than he'd imagined. Dr. Olivia Martin was a strikingly beautiful woman, but Olivia Martin was a knockout. She'd looked more like a college coed than a practicing physician, and she'd nearly knocked him off his feet.

Still, he'd managed to pull himself together long enough to discover that his new "wife" was the oldest of two daughters, that her father Jacob was a retired college English professor and her mother Grace raised prize-winning orchids. He'd learned her favorite movie was *Casablanca,* that she'd been fifteen when she'd gone out on her first date and that her grandparents owned the house just around the block from the one she'd grown up in. He knew what schools she had attended and what years she had graduated, what hospital she'd done her residency at and when she'd delivered her first baby. He'd also managed to find out she had a passion for chocolate and had more aunts, uncles, cousins and assorted other relatives than he'd ever be able to remember.

The last week hadn't been without its awkward moments, however. When she'd suddenly asked him his last name, he'd automatically told her the truth. Of course, it was egotistical to think she would connect Luke McCall, security guard with Lucas

McCall, CEO—egotistical to think that she'd even *heard* of him because it was embarrassingly obvious by her reaction that she had not. As far as she was concerned, his only motivation in taking the job was to earn a little extra money. And while he had to admit his vanity might have suffered a bruising, he wouldn't have relished the idea of having to explain why, if not for the money, he'd been willing to agree to pose as her husband, especially since he wasn't completely sure himself.

"Ladies and gentlemen, I'd like to welcome you aboard Coastal Airlines."

Lucas heard the powerful jet engines roar to life as the plane began its race down the runway. There would be no turning back now. After a brief layover in San Francisco, they would be landing in scenic Santa Barbara, California, and once they did, to Jacob and Grace Martin and the rest of the Martin family, he would be their newest member.

"You nervous?"

"Only about mixing up Aunt Kathleen with Aunt Kate or complimenting your mother on the roses instead of the...orchids, right?" He smiled as he opened his eyes and turned to her, but seeing the terrified look on her face, his smile quickly faded. "But I have a hunch you might be."

"I am," she confessed, sinking back against the seat. The plane shook with the fury of takeoff, sending a violent tremor through the aircraft. "Are we going to be able to pull this off?"

"Wait, wait, wait," he said, putting up a hand. "Weren't you the one reassuring me just a minute ago? Talk golf and roses and everything will be okay, remember?''

"Orchids."

"Whatever. You're supposed to be the optimistic one."

She clutched at the armrest with a death grip, peering out the small window of the plane as the runway passed in a blur. "It seemed a whole lot easier being optimistic on terra firma."

There was humor mingled with the nervousness, but there was also vulnerability and that surprised him. She'd always been so confident, so self-assured that the helplessness in her eyes caught him off guard. Before he had a chance to think, before he had a chance to question his motives or caution himself against it, he reacted. Reaching out, he slipped a comforting hand over hers on the armrest.

"Don't worry," he said, his fingers closing over her hand and giving it a reassuring squeeze. "Everything's going to be fine."

Suddenly they were off the ground, floating towards the clouds and leaving the violence and the trembling of the takeoff behind them.

"I hope you're right," she said, her gaze dropping to his hand on hers. "A lot depends on this."

He paused, following her line of vision. "You can tell me to mind my own business, but I have to confess, I'm curious about something."

She blinked, giving him a sidelong glance. "You mean other than me wanting to hire someone to pose as my husband for a week?"

"Well, yes, there is that," he admitted. "But I

can't help but wonder—why did you want your parents to think you'd gotten married?''

Olivia felt every muscle in her body go rigid. Of course she couldn't blame him for being curious. Who wouldn't be? Going to the lengths she had in order to affect such an elaborate hoax went way beyond crazy. It fell more in the range of certifiable. But she had her reasons, even if she couldn't—or wouldn't—tell him what they were. She had the baby to think about, the baby that belonged to her now, and that's what she had to keep reminding herself. Crazy or not, she had to do what she felt was best for everyone involved—her parents, her family and especially the baby. Besides, if Luke McCall knew the whole story, if he knew about Rachel and Ted and the arrangement they'd made, would it make the whole thing sound any less crazy to him?

"You know how parents can be," she said as casually as she could, hoping her voice didn't sound as strained as it felt in her throat. "Especially mothers. My folks are from that generation that thinks every woman has to have a man to take care of her. For the last ten years it's been 'When are you going to get married? All you do is work, work, work. When are you going to meet some nice man and settle down?' You know, that sort of thing.''

"So your parents are big believers in marriage, I take it?''

"Oh, yes.'' Olivia nodded, carefully slipping her hand from beneath his. "They just can't seem to understand I could be perfectly happy without a husband, that I love my career and I don't need a man to take care of me."

"So you told them you got married?"

Olivia tried to shift in her seat, but the seat belt held her snug. "I thought it would get them off my back for a while."

"You didn't think maybe they'd ever want to meet your husband?"

"Sure I did, but my parents refuse to fly and it's a long drive from Santa Barbara to Seattle. I figured by the time they got around to visiting, I'd be divorced." The seat belt sign finally snapped off and she flipped the clasp free. Leaning forward, she reached for the complimentary magazine from the pouch in front of her. "And a broken heart would probably buy me another couple of years of silence on the subject."

Luke was quiet for a moment, and she dared not look at him. She hoped the story didn't sound as ridiculous to him as it had to her.

"I guess that makes sense," he said after a moment. "Sort of."

"Oh." She settled back into her seat. If he thought it made sense—even sort of—maybe it wasn't so crazy. "Well, good."

He pulled a newspaper from the pocket of his jacket and opened it wide. "So I take it you've never been married?"

She flipped open the magazine. "No."

"Not even close?"

Olivia stared at a colorful advertisement on the page in front of her, but her mind was seeing the image of blond, blue-eyed Charles Latimer. She

thought of how starry-eyed she had been and how
naive. His practiced lines and slick evasiveness
seemed so painfully obvious to her now, but back
then the truth about his infidelity and his gigolo reputation had come as a crushing blow—a blow delivered with such relish from her own cousin. It had
been so crushing to her that it had sent her headlong
into her career, terrified of letting her heart feel anything again for fear of getting hurt.

Still, all that had been years ago. The hurt had
been long buried, long since put to rest. She no
longer really had an excuse to offer as to why there
was no one special in her life, except maybe that
she'd allowed her career to become the main focus
of her life. Still, all that was about to change with
the baby coming. Soon she would have a child to
think about, someone other than herself and her
needs to tend to and at three months into her pregnancy, she doubted if a man would consider her a
prime candidate for dating.

Without turning her head, she shot a sidelong
glance at Luke. Would he have been so willing to
meet her every evening in the doctor's lounge if
he'd known about the baby? Would their talks have
been so long? Would he have looked at her in the
same way?

"Not even close," she answered honestly, closing
the magazine and lowering it to her lap. "You?"

"Too close."

"Too close?" A cold chill shivered down her
spine. She'd just assumed he was single. He hadn't
looked married, hadn't *acted* married, but she of all
people should know that meant nothing. Charles

hadn't exactly acted married either. For all she knew Luke McCall could have a wife and ten kids back in Seattle. "Uh, how close is too close?"

He peered at her from over the top of his newspaper. "The divorce has been final for three years."

"Oh," she said with a nod. It was stupid to feel relieved, but she did. After all, she'd merely asked the man to be her husband, not marry her. "That close, huh?"

Luke smiled. "Yeah, that close."

"Any children?"

His smile disappeared. "No."

"Well, I suppose that's a blessing."

He lifted the newspaper. "I suppose," he said from behind the printed page.

Olivia picked up the magazine and began leafing through the pages again. Was it just her imagination or had he seemed a little sensitive about the subject of children? Had children played a part in the break-up of his marriage? It was really none of her business and had nothing to do with their "arrangement," but she couldn't help being curious. Still, if he had a problem with children—one way or the other—it was probably just as well he didn't know about the baby she was carrying. Being called upon to play the part of a proud father-to-be might just have proven too much for him.

"Would you like some coffee or tea. Maybe a soft drink?"

Olivia looked up at the young steward standing in the aisle behind a loaded beverage cart. Every nerve ending in her body cried for caffeine, but the doctor in her cautioned against it.

"Tea please. Herbal if you have it."

The steward smiled and nodded. "One herbal tea," he said, turning to Luke. "And you, sir?"

Luke reached forward and lowered the tray from the seat in front of him. "Coffee's fine for me thanks. Black."

The steward quickly went to work, pumping coffee from a shiny carafe into a cup for Luke, then pouring boiling water into a petite teapot and setting it on a tray with a cup and a packet of tea for her.

"Your coffee, sir," he said to Luke as he handed him a cup. "And herbal tea for your wife."

"See?" he whispered, shooting her a sly look. "We look married already."

Olivia reached for her tea, feeling ridiculously warm at the thought of looking like his wife. "Well, it's a start."

"Gotta start somewhere," he said, taking a healthy swallow of coffee.

She dropped the tea bag into the pot, watching while he took another drink. The aroma of his coffee made the sweet scent of her raspberry tea smell syrupy and woefully unappealing.

"Something the matter with the tea?" he asked when she made no move to pour herself a cup.

"No," she said, giving her head a shake. She couldn't tell him she would have sold her soul for a sip of his coffee, that it was only because of her pregnancy that she felt compelled to avoid it. "Just going to let it cool for a while."

He looked down at her cup and made a face. "I don't think cooling is going to help much."

She tried her best to look insulted. "What do you mean?"

He gave her a skeptical look. "You honestly like that stuff?"

"Sure," she lied, telling herself tiny white lies didn't count as being dishonest—not like telling your parents you'd gotten married when you really hadn't. "It's good for you."

"It might be good for you," he acknowledged dryly. "But it smells more like something you should be pouring over pancakes than drinking out of a cup."

"It's not that bad," she contended, but she didn't even sound convincing to herself.

"You don't drink coffee?"

"I tend to drink too much. That's why I switched to tea. I'm cutting down on caffeine."

"What for?"

"What do you mean what for?"

"Does it make you jumpy? Bother your sleep? What?"

"No," she said, remembering as an intern how she'd drink coffee all night long and then go home and fall dead asleep. "Because it's not good for you, that's why."

"Keep talking, Doc, you just might convince yourself."

She watched him take another sip of coffee, feeling her mouth salivate. "Caffeine is something we all should think about cutting out of our diets."

"If you're a heart patient maybe," he debated. "Or going to have a baby."

The remark caught her completely offguard,

causing her entire system to react and she jumped, sending tea sloshing over the sides of her cup.

"Whoa, whoa, careful or you'll burn yourself," he warned, plucking the cup from her hold. With a napkin, he dabbed at drops of tea that had spilled on the tray. "A little edgy, aren't you?"

"I'm fine," she mumbled, feeling heat rise in her cheeks. His comment about having a baby had been innocent, a coincidence really, but the fact that it had been right on target had completely unnerved her. "Just nervous."

"Relax," he advised in an overtly soothing voice that was full of amusement and good humor. Having cleaned the tray, he picked up her cup and carefully handed it to her again. "Everything's going to be fine. Just sit back and relax."

"I'm *trying* to relax," she told him, hoping she didn't sound as overwhelmed as she felt. "Which is exactly why I'm drinking herbal tea instead of coffee. The fact that it can make you very jittery is another good reason why you should stay away from it, you know."

"So all you doctors keep saying," he said, picking up his cup. "But judging from the way the coffee keeps disappearing out of the doctor's lounge, I'd say you're all either a bunch of hypocrites, or you just get a kick out of taking the joy out of your patients' lives."

"Well, we do enjoy that," she admitted, playing along and taking refuge in the easy teasing between them. "And while we all know patients know far more than their doctors, we still foolishly try to convince them from time to time that by taking a few precautions now—like exercising, eating right and cutting down on things like caffeine—they just might prevent some health problems later on.''

''So kind,'' Luke praised with a saccharine smile, raising the cup to his lips. ''You doctors are such angels.''

''And don't you feel bad having been so suspicious of our motives?'' she mocked in a wounded tone. She couldn't help notice how much younger he looked when he smiled, how much more relaxed and...how handsome. She appreciated his sense of humor and their joking had done more to relax her than any tea ever could.

''Oh, I do, I do,'' he admitted dryly, raising his cup. ''Well, bottoms up.''

''Here's to health,'' she toasted, raising her cup too, and thinking his laugh was about the nicest she'd heard. She swallowed a large gulp and groaned. ''Ugh, why is it that everything that's good for you has to taste like this?''

''Poor Doc,'' he laughed. ''The sacrifices you have to make for the sake of a good diet.''

''Okay, okay,'' she conceded, struggling not to laugh herself. ''I admit it, I hate the stuff.''

''You know,'' he said after a moment, his laughter subsiding. ''I could ask the steward to bring you a cup of coffee if you'd like.''

''No, no,'' she insisted, shaking her head. ''I'm going to finish this, whether I like it or not.''

He smiled as he watched her struggle with another sip. ''Stubborn, aren't you?''

''Not stubborn, just health conscious,'' she insisted, sipping again. ''You should try it sometime.''

"Would you care for a refill, sir?"

Luke glanced up at the steward and nodded. "Please."

"Walking time bomb," she warned as the steward filled his cup.

He glanced down into her sparkling eyes and felt something tighten in his chest. "Good thing I'm lucky then."

"Are you lucky?"

"Sure," he said, remembering how the sunlight had looked in her hair. "I'm married to a doctor." His smile turned mischievous as he reached for his cup. "Just don't tell Aunt Kate."

"Aunt Kathleen."

Her mischievous grin had the tension in his chest inch several degrees tighter. "I'm never going to remember."

Mother. Father. I'd like to introduce you to my husband.

Olivia squeezed her eyelids tight. Too formal, too impersonal. These were her parents. She needed something more affectionate, something more cute.

Hi, Mommy. Hi, Daddy. This is him. This is my new husband. Isn't he great?

She moaned. What was she, fifteen? Why didn't she just snap her gum and ask for the keys to the car while she was at it?

Opening her eyes, she glanced out the window of the plane. The landscape below was looking closer and more familiar and it wouldn't be long now before they were on the ground and she would be standing face-to-face with her parents.

Mr. and Mrs. Martin, this is Mr. McCall, my husband.

She rolled her eyes. Introductions were going to be awkward, that was a given, and she'd spent seven long days dreading them. If only she could come up with a plan, with an outline to follow or a format to focus on. She needed an opening line, something she could memorize, to hang on to so she wouldn't fumble and stumble and say something she would regret.

Mom. Dad. You two look great. Come say hi to my new hubby.

She sank back against the seat. Too bubbly, too animated.

She ran a hand across her eyes, pinching at the tension along the bridge of her nose. What was the matter with her? She'd always prided herself on her bedside manner, for knowing the right thing to say at the right time and for being able to put everyone at ease no matter how difficult the situation. But where was all that flair and ability now?

Hey you two—come give your new son-in-law a hug.

"Oh, help," she groaned, leaning forward and burying her face in her hands.

Luke had been napping, but he opened his eyes now and stretched as best as he could given the cramped conditions. "You okay?"

Olivia spread her fingers apart, peeking up at him from the spaces in between. "I don't think so."

"Ladies and gentlemen," the voice announced over the plane's P.A. system. "The seat belt sign has now come on in preparation for our landing in Santa Barbara."

She closed her fingers, and groaned again.

"Don't be nervous." He reached out and gently pulled her hands from her face. "Sit back and try and relax a little. Everything's going to be fine."

"That's easy for you to say," she mumbled, sinking back into the seat as the steward rushed down the aisle, securing compartments and checking seat belts.

"I don't think so," he protested. "I'm the one who should be nervous."

"You?" She turned and looked up at him. "What have you got to be worried about?"

"You mean other than keeping Chris straight from Kristin and Aunt Kate from Aunt Kathleen and Poo Poo from Pee Pee."

"Poo Paw."

He tossed his hands in the air. "See what I mean?"

"But in a week it will be all over for you."

He hesitated for a moment, watching again how the sunlight through the tiny window moved through her hair as the plane turned for its final approach. "Except then I'll be the bad guy."

"Bad guy?"

The plane lurched suddenly and their hands brushed as they both clutched for the armrest. "Yeah, then I'll be the jerk who broke their daughter's heart."

Chapter Three

"Is that them over there?"

Olivia peered through the crowd. "Where?"

Luke pointed again. "Over there on the walk—the couple waving?"

She spotted her parents and a lump of emotion swelled so large in her throat that it threatened to choke her. What on earth was she doing? She'd never lied to her parents before—she loved them. How could she deceive and mislead them?

She could feel Luke's hand at the center of her back as they made their way out of the plane, down the portable stairway and across the tarmac towards the gate. She remembered how he had placed his hand over hers on the plane and how they'd touched again when they'd both grabbed at the armrest at the same time.

It wasn't actually something she'd given much thought to but somewhere in her brain she'd as-

sumed that if they were ever going to convince people they were married, some touching would have
to be involved. She just hadn't planned on how she
might react. His hand against hers felt stable and
steady, and she found herself taking comfort in it.
He was so calm—she was a wreck! Her stiff, leaden
legs felt awkward and carried her in a clumsy, jerky
motion. If he was nervous, it certainly didn't show.
Luke McCall either had nerves of steel, or he was
one hell of an actor.

"Well it's about time," Grace Martin said, rushing forward and wrapping her arms around her
daughter. Pulling back, her lip quivered with emotion and huge tears rolled down her cheeks. "I
swear, I didn't think that plane was ever going to
get here."

"All right, Mother, that's enough, that's
enough," Jacob Martin scolded, stepping in between
them and handing his wife a handkerchief. Turning
to Olivia, he opened his arms. "Now come give
your old man a squeeze before she really turns on
the waterworks."

Olivia felt overwhelmed with emotion. A man uncomfortable with public displays of affection, her
father hugged her so tight she could hardly catch her
breath. The embrace had expressed more to her than
any words ever could. Pulling away, he abruptly set
her away from him and turned away, but not before
she caught a glimpse of the tears in his eyes too.

"We, uh, probably should be heading over to the
baggage claim," he mumbled in a low voice.

"Oh, Jacob," Grace scolded, dabbing at her eyes

with the handkerchief. "For pity sake, give them a chance to catch their breath."

Olivia realized with numbing clarity that the time had indeed come. There they were, standing all together—face-to-face. This was it, the moment she had been dreading, her Waterloo, her Armageddon, her moment of truth—only for her there would be no truth. Everyone was looking to her to do something, to take a step forward and get the ball rolling, to open her mouth and say something.

Only…there was nothing. She opened her mouth, but nothing came out—not a word, not a scream, not even one of those ridiculous stock phrases she'd been rehearsing. She just stood there, frozen by fear and rendered mute by panic.

"It was nice of you both to come meet us."

Luke's voice penetrated the canyons of her brain and bounced through it like an echo. While she stood there like a stick, he calmly reached around her, extending a hand to her father and giving her mother a hug. Like something out of a surreal dream, she watched the action play out around her, unable to hear for the ringing in her ears and only half believing what it was she was seeing. The three of them stood there together, chatting and laughing like old friends.

"I have to admit I've been a little nervous at the prospect of meeting Olivia's parents," he admitted, glancing back in her direction and winking. "But she kept telling me to relax."

"Well she was right," Grace said, slipping an arm through his as he escorted her down the walk and towards the green and white striped tent that served as a makeshift baggage claim at the tiny airport. "And if the truth be known, we were a little nervous ourselves. I mean, you two eloping like that took us by surprise."

"I hope you weren't too upset," Luke said.

"Maybe a little at first," she confessed, looking up at him and giving him a sly smile. "But we're getting used to the idea."

The smile Luke gave her mother was so charming Olivia felt its effect despite the distance between them. She was amazed by him. They'd been there less than ten minutes and yet he'd already won over her mother and, by the way staid and restrained Professor Martin was beaming, Luke was well on his way to winning him over too. She hardly considered herself a snob and knew better than to judge a book by its cover, but she couldn't help wondering what he had done in his life and where he had been to develop such polish and easy sophistication. Was all the flash and polish just part of the act? How much of what he was showing was illusion, and how much of it was real?

"I'll warn you though," Grace continued, turning to Olivia as Luke pulled their bags from the baggage carrier. "It's a little frantic back at the house. Of course with the reception being in the backyard, we've been working day and night on the garden. You know, of course, that Sam and Robyn are living up here now—I told you that didn't I? Well, anyway I have to say, they have been so sweet coming over evenings and on weekends to help out. Sam wanted to get as much done before Kathleen arrived because..." She stopped, giving Olivia a knowing look. "Well, you know."

Olivia did know and, from his expression it was obvious Luke knew too. It was ridiculous to feel pleased, but she did. Apparently he'd not only listened during the crash course she'd given him on her family, but he'd managed to remember some of it as well.

"And the wedding coordinator is coming over again this afternoon to help us try to decide how to set up the tables," Grace proceeded as they followed Jacob towards the parking lot. "Monica and I had thought maybe two long tables along the walk, but the coordinator is suggesting several round tables clustered around the lawn, what do you think?"

It took Olivia a moment to realize her mother had asked her a question. Flustered, she gave her head a shake. "I, uh, d-don't know."

"Well, she wanted to set up a few here and there this afternoon to give us an idea, but I warned her we wouldn't have much time. We've all got fittings this afternoon and— Oh!" She stopped abruptly, watching as Jacob started down a long row of parked cars. "For heaven's sake will you look at that? Where is that man going?" She rolled her eyes, marching across the lot towards him. "No. Not down there. Jacob! Row A. We're in Row A."

Olivia watched the two of them together and felt another swell of emotion rise in her throat.

"Relax."

It was Luke's nearness that had Olivia jump more than the sound of his whispered voice in her ear.

She whirled around so fast, she brought them practically nose-to-nose.

"Don't look so worried," he continued. His gaze moved from her to Grace and Jacob, his chin bobbing in their direction. "They're terrific. Everything is going fine." He turned to Olivia again. "Relax."

Relax. She wasn't sure that was possible. Still, he was right. Things were going fine, far better than she would have expected in fact, but if she didn't loosen up a little, her parents really would start getting suspicious.

Mind over matter, she said herself. If she acted married, her parents would believe she was married. Maybe if she acted relaxed they'd believe that too. Straightening her shoulders, she ran a damp palm along her skirt.

"Relax," she mumbled, taking a cleansing breath. "I'm relaxed."

"Atta girl," Luke praised as they started across the lot again.

"We're here. Over here," Grace shouted, waving at them over the tops of a line of cars. As they neared, she put her hands on her hips. "I swear your father would have had us walking all over this lot."

Olivia actually found herself laughing. It felt good to laugh, felt good to know she could.

"Dad has a bit of a reputation when it comes to parking lots," she said, turning to Luke. "He has a bad habit of forgetting where he parked."

"Don't you be listening to this one," Jacob warned him in a good-natured tone. "She and her sister and mother like nothing better than to give this poor old man grief." He opened the trunk of his late model sedan and deposited a suitcase inside. "The stories I could tell you."

"But you won't, will you, dear?" Grace said with saccharine sweetness, giving him a loving tap on the shoulder.

Jacob looked up at Luke and shrugged. "See what I mean? I don't mind telling you I'm glad there will be a bit more male blood in this family. I've been outnumbered for too long. Time to even up the odds just a little."

"Except when it comes to a woman," Luke said, lifting the rest of the luggage into the trunk and lowering the lid. "I'm not sure you can ever even up those odds."

Jacob Martin laughed, slipping an arm around Olivia's shoulders. "I think this new husband of yours is a very wise man."

"Or maybe just one who likes to live dangerously," Luke quickly added, reaching out and plucking Olivia on the nose.

Olivia felt her face flush with color. It had been such an innocent gesture, but one that spoke of familiarity and affection, and she wasn't sure how to react.

"I think the safest bet is just to forget the odds and do whatever you're told," she advised, hoping they would contribute the stiffness in her voice to sarcasm and wit and not suspect how awkward she really felt.

"You will never know, my boy," Jacob said, making a play of sounding weary. "You have *no* idea how complicated life can be when you're the lone man in a household full of women."

"The only sane voice in a world of chaos?" Luke offered innocently, opening the door of the car and making a sweeping gesture to Olivia.

"The only light in a very, very dark tunnel," Jacob confirmed, opening the other door and gallantly making the same gesture for Grace.

"They're *so* clever," Grace said to Olivia as she slipped into the front seat of the car.

"Aren't they though," Olivia agreed, taking Luke's proffered hand and letting him help her into the back seat of the car.

Grace watched as Jacob and Luke rounded the car, turning to Olivia in the seat behind her, eyes sparkling. "Oh, sweetheart, I think he's wonderful."

Lucas waited until Olivia was safely buckled into her seat belt in the back of the car, then firmly closed the door. Even though he had the whole rest of her family left to meet, he couldn't help feeling he'd made it over a major hurdle. Olivia's parents were lovely people, but he understood how they could present an undaunting presence. Jacob Martin may have a wry, acerbic wit he could appreciate, but his stern expression and icy blue eyes had no doubt put the fear of God into the hearts of many a teenage boy who'd been brave enough to cross his threshold to take out one of his daughters. And Grace Martin's warm, affable smile and bubbly nature didn't mask a shrewd eye that let little escape. Where Jacob might wonder just how a man would support his daughter, it would be Grace who would study him with keen perception and size up the man's character.

Rounding the car, he glanced through the window at Grace and gave her a wink. He was never one to jump to conclusions, but early evidence would suggest that so far she'd found his character intact.

"Smooth flight?"

Lucas looked up, peering over the top of the car at Jacob. "It was a little bumpy landing in San Francisco, but the flight here was smooth as silk." He walked around the car to where Jacob stood. "It was beautiful coming in—the ocean, the mountains. Very scenic."

Jacob surveyed the almost cloudless sky overhead. "It's clear today, but we were socked in earlier in the week. Pea soup." He jingled the car keys he held in his hand. "Ever been down this way before?"

Lucas shook his head. "Never, but from what I've seen, I like it."

Jacob reached for the driver's door. "Tell me, Lucas, you much of a golfer?"

Lucas had to smile. "I've been known to find my way around a course."

Jacob's eyes widened. "Really."

"Of course, we get a lot of rain up in our area," Lucas continued with a modest shrug. "And sinking a fifteen-foot putt in a full downpour may not be easy, but I assure you it can be done."

"Is that so?" Jacob said thoughtfully, his smile broadening. He let his gaze drop to the two women in the car. "I suppose it would raise quite a ruckus if we were to swing by the country club sometime this afternoon."

"I don't imagine that idea would go over very

well," Lucas conceded, following his line of vision. "But like I said before, there are those of us who like to live dangerously."

"Yep," Jacob mumbled with a laugh as he pulled the door open. "A pretty smart fella."

Lucas smiled and climbed into the back seat next to Olivia. She didn't look nearly as nervous as she had earlier and for some reason that made him feel better. She had looked so overwrought and anxious when they'd gotten off the plane he'd forgotten about his own apprehension. He'd just wanted to do what he could to help ease her burden just a little, to help smooth the way so she would be free to relax.

He turned and looked out the window, glancing at the row of palms lining Goleta Beach as Jacob maneuvered the car on to Clarence Ward Drive, heading towards Highway 101. There had been such panic in Olivia's blue eyes when she'd stepped off that plane—the blue eyes she had inherited from her father. But Olivia Martin was a strong, independent woman and he had to stop thinking of her as helpless. One way or another he was going to have to stop himself from trying to rescue a woman who was more than capable of saving herself.

Still, she had been nervous about facing her parents and now, after having met them, he could understand why she didn't feel right about not being completely truthful with them. It was obvious it was something she wasn't used to doing.

He turned, seeing only confidence in her blue eyes now. It puzzled him, though, as to why she had felt the need to tell them she was married. What she had said about her family pressuring her to settle down made sense, but it seemed like such an elaborate ruse just to keep them from pestering her about it, especially knowing how obviously difficult it was for her to deceive them.

"So tell me, Lucas," Grace said, turning as far around in her seat as the restraining belt would allow. "How did your family react to the news of your marriage? Were your parents surprised?"

Lucas watched Olivia's expression stiffen. His family wasn't something they'd discussed.

"Actually, there's just my mom and my brother," he said, shifting his gaze to Grace. That was the truth. "And I think their reaction was probably a lot like yours—shock." That wasn't. He glanced at Olivia. "I guess we surprised a lot of people."

"And I suspect that's somewhat of an understatement," Grace added dryly. "Olivia's told us nothing of your family, so you have just the one brother? Is he in Seattle too?"

Lucas nodded. "He sure is. Actually Linc works for m..." He stopped abruptly, momentarily flustered. He'd very nearly blurted out too much. "He, uh, works in security downtown."

"And your mother? Is she close by?"

"Bellevue, just across the lake."

"And I'm sure you visit her often?"

Lucas laughed, understanding now where she was going with this. "Not as often as she thinks I should, but I try to get over there when I can."

"Well your mother is lucky to have both her children close, I envy her." She shot Olivia a look that was as affectionate as it was disapproving. "My daughter the doctor has a nasty habit of forgetting about her parents." She glanced back to Lucas. "She telephones about as often as she visits."

"That's not true," Olivia insisted.

"Oh, that's right, I forgot," Grace mocked. "There was that call last Christmas."

"I'm not that bad." Olivia leaned forward, giving her mother a playful swat on the arm. "And you seem to forget I have a practice to run. That does take up a considerable amount of my time."

"So you keep reminding us. I'm just glad you finally managed to find time for a few other things." Grace turned to Lucas. "For a long time all this woman ever did was work. I'm counting on you, Lucas, not to let that happen anymore."

"I'll do my best," he assured her.

"And while you're at it, you might try and convince her to start delivering a few of her own babies instead of everyone else's."

"Mother!"

Lucas could see Olivia's face flood with color, and thinking about her carrying his child had him feeling a little flushed himself.

"Shoot me for wanting to be a grandmother before I hit the century mark," Grace said, holding up her hands in surrender.

"Don't tempt me," Olivia warned. "And now if you're through poking your nose into places it doesn't belong, can we talk about the wedding? You told me about the tables in the garden, but what was that again about striped tents? And what about her dress? When do I get a chance to see Monica's dress?''

"Well, like I said, we have fittings this afternoon at three o'clock so you'll be able to see it then," Grace said, her curiosity with her new son-in-law temporarily interrupted by the excitement evident in her voice. "And you're going to love it, I know. It's so beautiful. She also is having the photographer meet us there to shoot a few informal pictures for her scrapbook and—"

Lucas watched mother and daughter excitedly planning for the big event. Listening while she filled Olivia in on all the plans and preparations, he found himself getting caught up with them too.

"Speaking of shooting," Jacob said, interrupting her and surprising everyone. "Lucas and I were thinking while you girls were out this afternoon trying on your dresses we might—"

"Jacob Martin," Grace advised in a tone that would brook no resistance. "If what you're about to propose has anything—even remotely—to do with shooting a round of golf this afternoon, I would *strongly* suggest you not say it."

Jacob glanced in the rearview mirror at Lucas and shrugged. Turning to his wife, he smiled sweetly. "Say what, my dear?"

"Oh, look at that," Grace groaned as Jacob turned on to the long tree-shrouded drive leading to their ranch-style house. "Kathleen and Maury are here. I didn't think they'd get here until this evening."

Olivia leaned forward, pointing out the window. "Then whose sports car is that?"

"Oh, that's Kristin's little car. She and her mother decided to drive up early," Grace said, following her line of vision.

"Poo Paw's here?" Olivia asked, shooting Lucas a look and smiling. "That's my Aunt Anne."

"Poo Paw," he murmured, rolling his eyes.

"Poo Paw is here," Grace laughed. "Jake and Chris will fly in for the wedding, but Anne wanted to come up and help Katherine with Monica's shower—it's tomorrow night, you know. She told me they'd come by early today to say hello, have a chance to meet Lucas before things got too hectic."

"Well I think she can forget about that now," Jacob pointed out. "With Kathleen and Maury's boys, things are likely to be pretty hectic from now on."

Lucas listened as Olivia and her parents kidded and joked about their various family members, their teasing endearing rather than critical. It was clear this was a family who cared about one another—warts and all.

"Oh, Lucas," Grace sighed as Jacob brought the car to a stop in front of the house. "All this must sound pretty awful to you. You must think we're terrible."

"No," he insisted. "I think you sound like a family."

"A bunch of crazies, if you ask me," Jacob muttered, pushing his door open and stepping out on to the drive.

"I don't remember anyone asking you that, dear," Grace called to him before he closed the door. Gathering up her purse, she turned to Luke. "Sometime you make Olivia tell you about my sister Kathleen and the screwy thing that happened at her daughter's wedding."

"Actually, she has," he said, looking at Olivia and nodding. "And I've been given strict instructions to steer clear of the subject of lawn maintenance."

"I'd say that's very wise advice," Grace said, shooting her daughter a look. "And I'm glad to know your wife has told you something about her family since she neglected to tell us anything about you."

"Mother," Olivia complained. "Don't start that again."

"Oh, I won't," Grace said breezily, pushing her car door open. "I've got a whole week to find all that out for myself."

Lucas knew she was teasing but given the circumstances, the thought of having to answer questions about himself and his "marriage" to Olivia wasn't something he looked forward to.

Alone in the car, he glanced at Olivia, leaning close. "Why do I feel like I should run home and do my homework?"

"Probably for the same reason I feel like I just found out there's going to be a quiz in the morning."

"Come on you two," Grace called, rapping on the window. "We don't have enough time for smooching."

Lucas looked at Olivia and they both started laughing.

"You ready?" he asked, seeing a hint of apprehension mingled with the excitement in her eyes.

She drew in a deep breath. "As ready as I'll ever be."

They had barely stepped out of the car when a loud scream from inside the house had everyone looking up. Almost instantly, the front door flew open and a young woman leaped out of the house and ran across the drive towards them. Lucas needed no introduction to know that this was Monica—the bride-to-be.

"Ooolliiiveeeaaa," Monica squealed, her voice trailing after her like the tail of a kite as she ran across the drive. "You're here. I can't believe it. You're *here*."

The resemblance between the two sisters was unmistakable, and yet they each had their own unique take on the beauty they shared. Monica's short cropped hair shone red in the sunlight, making Olivia's long golden strands look even paler, and while Olivia stood at least two inches taller than her sister, they shared the same blue eyes and slender build.

The two sisters collapsed into each other's arms, laughter mingling with tears, screams with snivels. They seemed able to communicate through all the emotion, but Lucas could make nothing out of what they were saying. He only knew he'd become the topic of discussion when they both turned and rushed towards him.

"Oh, Lucas," Monica sobbed by way of an introduction. She wrapped her arms around his neck. "Oh, Lucas, I'm so happy."

Suddenly there was a stream of people pouring out of the house and encircling him. Somehow they all managed to get transported from the drive, up the steps and inside the house, but the next thirty minutes were a blur of names and faces and hugs and handshakes for him. He scrambled to put faces together with names, but it was a losing battle.

He barely had a chance to look at the house Olivia Martin had grown up in, but somewhere in the midst of the madness and confusion of names and faces, he managed to get the impression of a warm and comfortable home. The Martins were not wealthy people, but their two story ranch-style house nestled on a five-acre plot at the base of San Marcos Pass was far from modest. With the small grove of avocado trees, rolling hills and wide open spaces, he could only imagine it would have been a terrific place to grow up—a far cry from the run-down apartment he'd been forced to live in with his mother and brother after his father had deserted them.

Life hadn't been easy back then. Working two jobs to keep a roof over their heads, his mother had been gone almost constantly. At eight years old, the responsibility of cooking and cleaning and taking care of five-year-old Linc fell on his young shoulders, which left little time for a kid to be a kid. A lot had changed in their lives since those bleak days, but memories of that harsh past were something that would be with them always. The scars went deep, but so did the love. The first thing he had done when his business had begun making money was to buy his mother a luxury penthouse condominium. He believed she was happy now, and he made damn sure she wanted for nothing. No amount of money could make up for the pain and the hardships of those dark days, but he could make sure they would never come back.

"Lucas dear," Grace called over the din of the others. "Have Olivia show you where to put those bags up in her old room. The wedding coordinator is going to be here soon and you two need to get into some cooler clothes. You're back in California now, we live in the sunshine."

Olivia looked from her mother, to Lucas, then back to her mother again. "My old room?"

"I thought you'd be more comfortable in there. Kathleen and Maury will be in the guest room and I thought Kevin and Joseph could camp out in the den. Monica offered to let the boys use her room, but I hated to do that. She's only going to be home for a few more nights, I didn't want to think of her sleeping on the sofa the night before her wedding."

"No, no," Olivia insisted, shaking her head. "The boys can use my room. Lucas and I are staying at a hotel."

"A hotel?"

Grace's horrified gasp silenced the entire living room.

"We...we have reservations," Olivia mumbled, awkward with all eyes on her. She turned to Lucas. "Right?"

Lucas saw the desperation in her eyes again. The two rooms they'd reserved at a nearby hotel had been intended as a convenient way to avoid any embarrassment over "sleeping arrangements," but it was hardly something they could share with the rest of the family.

"Right," he added, turning to Grace. "And you've got a full house already."

"That's nonsense," Grace scoffed.

"And we've already made the arrangements," Olivia added.

"Absolutely not, your father and I insist—" Grace began, shaking her head.

"No, no, no," Aunt Kathleen said, making her way across the crowded living room and interrupting them both. "If anyone is moving to a hotel, it's Maury and the boys and me." She turned to Olivia. "We don't want to put you out."

"No one is being put out," Grace insisted.

"Of course not," Monica added, leaping up off the sofa and running towards them. "There's my room. I can crash on the sofa, it's no big deal."

"That is not going to be necessary," Grace contended, her voice growing loud.

"You're right, it's not going to be necessary," Olivia explained. "Because Luke and I have already decided."

"I won't hear of it," Kathleen said, shaking her head as well. "We don't mind one bit."

"Better yet, why don't I just get a hotel room," Monica suggested. "It's just for a few days and it would be so much easier."

"No," Grace said adamantly, growing visibly upset. "You are not checking into a hotel."

"That's right," Kathleen agreed. "Because Maury and I are."

Grace turned to her sister and shook her head again. "No you are not! I insist that you stay. I *want* you to."

"But dear, if there's not room—"

"There's plenty of room," Grace said, desperation causing her voice to inch up another degree. "Olivia, tell your Aunt Kathleen there is plenty of room."

Olivia gave Lucas a dismal look that had his breath catching in his lungs. It was there again in her eyes, that uncharacteristic helplessness, that total vulnerability that had him wanting to ride in on his white horse and save her. The situation was quickly moving from bad to worse and it wouldn't be long before they were all in tears.

"There's plenty of room, Aunt Kathleen," she said dutifully.

"But Maury and I wouldn't mind," Kathleen said. "I know what it means to your parents to have you here and we would feel terrible if we thought we forced you to go to a hotel."

"No one is going to a hotel," Grace announced in a weary voice. "Lucas, say you're not going to a hotel."

Lucas hardly remembered taking that step forward, but like a hang glider leaping from a cliff, he jumped into the fray. "Of course, we'd love to stay." He turned to Olivia and shrugged. "Right?"

"Right, of course," she said struggling to smile, but her voice sounded anything but enthusiastic.

"Good," Grace said with a loud clap of her hands and a tremendous sigh of relief. "Then it's all settled. Everyone is staying." She pointed to the bags in the entry and turned to Olivia and Lucas. "Now why don't you two put your bags upstairs and get changed. We've got a busy afternoon."

Chapter Four

Olivia stepped through the doorway and into the bedroom of her childhood, feeling a little as though she were stepping back in time. The walls were littered with pictures and posters, and the bookshelves were crammed with mementos of a little girl who had grown to womanhood. She walked across the room, running a hand along the top of the dresser and along the edge of the bed as she passed. There were the ballet slippers she had worn in her first grade dance recital, the pom-poms she had used as a cheerleader in junior high and the autographed picture of a teen-idol she had waited two hours in line to get. There was even the dried corsage Jim Ryan had given her when he'd taken her to the San Marcos High School senior prom.

She swallowed, her throat choked with emotion. Everywhere she looked, everything she touched brought back a flood of memories—good memories, wonderful memories of a childhood spent loved and feeling secure. Everyone deserved a childhood like that, filled with warm memories and good feelings and yet she knew that didn't happen very often. She had been very lucky to have had wonderful parents, to have grown up feeling protected in a warm, stable home and to have memories she could cherish, but she wasn't sure she'd fully appreciated that until this moment. She wanted to give the baby growing inside of her the kind of love and security she had known, the kind Rachel and Ted would have given their child had they lived.

"Where would you like me to put these?"

Olivia jumped at the sound of Luke's voice behind her. Turning around, she swiped at the tear making its way down her cheek.

He stood in the doorway looking at her. Luke. It was the name that had been stitched across the badge of his uniform, the name she had always called him. Luke McCall, security guard. But when he had introduced himself to her parents he had referred to himself as Lucas. Lucas McCall. The name had sounded so different to her then—different and yet oddly familiar. It wasn't exactly a common name, but it wasn't particularly unusual either. Yet there had been something when she'd heard him say it, something that had registered in the back of her brain. Was it just her imagination playing tricks on her, or had she heard that name before?

"Oh," she said, rushing to the louvered closet doors and pulling them open. "Right in here is fine."

He stepped inside the room and walked to the

closet, his tall frame and broad shoulders swallowing up the space and leaving the room feeling
cramped and confining.

"Nice room," he said after he'd settled the bags
in the closet and looked about. Glancing out the
window, he gestured with a bob of his chin. "Nice
view of the mountains too."

She turned, following his line of vision, and gazed
out the window she had stared out a million times
before. "It is pretty."

He slowly moved about the room, studying the
books on the shelves and the memorabilia scattered
about and Olivia found herself growing more uncomfortable. Her entire childhood was there, things
about herself she wasn't sure she wanted him to see.

"I'm, uh, I'm sorry about this," she said in an
effort to distract him.

He looked up from the poster he'd been studying.
"There's nothing for you to feel sorry about."

She watched as he turned from the poster and
picked up the small porcelain thimble her Aunt Kate
had brought her from Washington D.C. "But this
makes things a lot more awkward." He put the thimble down and reached for a small piece of cardboard
Jim Ryan had scribbled a note to her on after he'd
made the winning touchdown at the high school
homecoming game. She could see the scrawled let-
ters in her mind—*Now will you go out with me?*
"Not exactly what we'd planned."

"Plans change," he said, looking up from having
read the paper and putting it back on the shelf.

"But sharing a room…" She caught a glimpse of
her four-poster bed with its flowered dust ruffle and

stuffed animals from the corner of her eye and the words died on her lips.

"You were saying?"

She turned to him, confused. "What?"

"You were saying something about sharing a room?"

"Oh, right!" She gave her head a shake, hoping he couldn't see the heat she could feel in her cheeks. "Yes, sharing a room—it doesn't give us very much privacy."

He glanced up from the framed picture of her and Monica he'd been studying on the wall. "Maybe not, but we're both adults." He gave her a little half smile. "And I think I can trust you to behave yourself."

"Well, I don't doubt that we ca—"

"Who is this?" he asked, pointing at the youthful entertainer whose picture was inside the frame. "David Crosby or Cosby, or something like that?"

"Cassidy," she corrected, giving her head a shake. "And it's Shaun Cassidy."

"Oh, right, Shaun Cassidy," he repeated after her, pointing a finger at the face in the picture. He stopped, peering close and studying the writing scrawled across the glossy print. "What's he got written on here? To Olivia, my..." He shook his head. "I can't make it out. Is that m-u-m-l Mumble? Or maybe numb..."

"Number," she said testily. She stomped across the room, pointing to each word in the inscription. "It's number. My-number-one-fan. I was Shaun Cassidy's number one fan."

If her outburst had surprised him, it didn't show

in his expression. He turned to look at her, his face smiling in amusement. "You liked this guy?"

"It was a long time ago," she explained with an exasperated sigh, walking back to the window. "I was thirteen years old. And what I was saying about the room was—"

"What was it, at a concert or something?" he asked, interrupting her again.

"Yes, a concert," she said, making no attempt to hide the annoyance out of her voice. "He was at the Bowl."

"The Bowl?"

"The Santa Barbara Bowl," she snapped, her voice growing loud. She was trying to discuss something important here, so why were they talking about Shaun Cassidy? "Luke, I wanted to say—"

"So were you one of those little girls screaming in the audience?"

The man was being impossible and Olivia was ready to strangle him. "I was a teenybopper, okay? I went to his concert, I screamed my head off and I waited two hours in line to get that lousy autograph. Is there anything else you want to know? What songs he sang, what dress I was wearing, the color lipstick I had on?"

He reacted this time, straightening up and looking a little like she'd just landed a right along his jaw. "Olivia, is there something wrong?"

"Something wrong?" Olivia sputtered. "You mean other than the fact that I've been trying to discuss something important with you and all you seem interested in is some silly David Cassidy concert I went to a lifetime ago."

He looked at her, then to the picture on the wall, then back to her again. "I thought you said it was Shaun?"

"I thought—" she began in an artificially calm voice, wondering if steam could indeed come out of a person's ears "—maybe we should discuss—"

"I'll just make a bed on the floor," he said, cutting her off. He crossed the room to where she stood. "We'll work it out, don't worry."

She looked up into his eyes and felt the irritation and frustration evaporate. "It just makes it so awkward."

"It doesn't have to be, not if we're considerate of each other and I think we can be. Besides, you saw what happened just now with your mother and your aunt. If we'd insisted on going to a hotel, then it really would have made things awkward."

He was right, of course, but it still wasn't going to make the next six days any easier. Sharing a room with the man wasn't exactly what she'd had in mind when she'd asked him to play the part of her husband.

"I feel embarrassed," she confessed. "It is rather above and beyond the scope of our agreement."

"The agreement was to be your husband," he said simply. "And husbands and wives share bedrooms."

He was right about that. It was just that she was finding the whole charade more difficult than she'd expected. She had to keep reminding herself that what she was doing would simply be better for everyone in the long run—the baby, her parents and the entire family.

"I know," she said with a sigh. "You're right. And I really do appreciate you being so understanding about..." She looked around the small room, making a sweeping gesture with her arms. "Well, about all this."

"Well hey," he said, walking back across the room to the picture hanging on the wall. "How many times do you get a chance to sleep in a room with an autographed picture of Shaun Cassidy on the wall?"

They were both laughing when the rap on the door had them both jumping.

"Are you decent?" Grace called from the hall.

"Hardly decent," Lucas said, pulling the door open. "But we're dressed."

Grace stepped inside, looking curiously contrite. "I know it's not a luxury hotel room, but it isn't so bad, is it?"

"It's wonderful," Lucas assured her. Smiling, he pointed to the window. "And it comes with a million dollar view."

Grace shifted her gaze to Olivia, then back to Lucas. "Then you're not upset with me?"

"Upset?" Lucas's smile disappeared. He slipped a comforting arm around her shoulders. "Why should we be upset?"

"Jacob says I pressured you too much about staying. You are newlyweds, after all, and if you want to be alone I'll understand." She looked up at him. "I really will."

"Oh, that's silly, Mom," Olivia insisted, crossing the room and gathering her mother's hands in hers.

"Of course it is," Lucas agreed. "And it wasn't that we didn't want to stay."

"Lucas is right, Mom," Olivia said, giving her mother's hands a squeeze. "We didn't want to go to a hotel. We just wanted to make things easier for you."

"I appreciate it," Grace said, looking from one to the other. "I really do. But I love having you here and I so wanted my whole family under one roof. I hope you'll understand."

"We do," Olivia assured her, not entirely comfortable having to defend the decision but helpless to do anything else.

"Well, good," Grace said, giving them both a hug. "I didn't want you to be angry. And I know the bed is a little narrow, but you can just cuddle up, right?"

"Right," Lucas said. When he turned to Olivia and winked, she felt her entire body go weak.

Grace turned, starting for the door. "Well, I'll leave you two alone now. You get changed and come downstairs. You're never going to believe who just knocked at the door."

"The wedding coordinator?" Olivia asked.

"Oh, you'll see," Grace sang, floating around the corner and out of sight.

"Surprise, Olivia!"

"Sherry?"

Lucas didn't have to see Olivia's face to know her reaction to seeing her cousin, he could hear it in the sound of her voice.

"W-what are you doing here?" she stammered.

"What am I doing here?" Sherry repeated, motioning Olivia down with her hand. "Where else would I be?"

It was obvious to Lucas that Olivia couldn't move. She stood rooted to her spot at the top of the stairs. Slowly stepping up behind her, he carefully guided her down the stairs and into the foyer. He could feel the tension in her body and felt himself grow tense as well. He remembered what she had said about Sherry, about her poking and prodding and reminded himself to be on guard.

"But you weren't suppose to..." Olivia shook her head. "I mean, I thought you were—"

"On a cruise ship, I know, I know," Sherry finished for her with an animated laugh. She reached out an arm and leaned forward, kissing at the air as she gave Olivia a half-hug. "But you didn't think a little thing like three thousand miles and a boat load of passengers was going to stop me from being here to see Monica get married." With an almost inelegant shove, she pushed past Olivia and turned to him. "Or from meeting your new husband, did you?" Looking up at him, her dark burgundy lips parted in a brilliant smile. "You must be the wonderful Lucas I keep hearing about."

"I don't know how wonderful," he said modestly, taking her outstretched hand. There was nothing subtle about the woman's overdone makeup or the generous measure of cleavage she displayed. Their message came through loud and clear; she was a woman determined to get attention any way that she could. "But I am Lucas. Lucas McCall."

"And I'm Sherry Phillips," she purred, bypassing his hand and looping her arm through his. "Hello, cousin."

And there was nothing subtle about the way her very copious breasts brushed his arm as she pulled him close. Still, he suspected the sultry look she gave him was more for Olivia's benefit than for his, but smiled down at her anyway.

It wasn't too terribly difficult to understand what was going on, that cousin Sherry wanted to get a rise out of Olivia, to make her jealous. Of course the woman had no way of knowing her efforts were in vain. He and Olivia were, after all, only pretending to be man and wife and no amount of flirting was going to make his *wife* jealous.

"Olivia, I'm going to steal this gorgeous husband of yours," Sherry purred, turning to Lucas and pulling him by the arm. "Why don't we go into the living room where we can relax and have a nice long chat. I just want to hear everything about how you and dear old Olivia met. I mean, I swear we didn't think that girl was ever going to get married, but I guess she fooled us. From what I understand, it was love at first sight."

Lucas gave Olivia a quick glimpse as Sherry dragged him past. She looked more angry now than nervous and he found himself smiling. It was ridiculous given the circumstances, but the thought that Olivia might feel even a little possessive of him felt good.

"At first sight," he confirmed, his smile growing wide. He turned to Sherry as she steered him through the living room towards the sofa. "At least it was for me."

"Oh, that's just too romantic," Sherry sighed, sinking down on to the soft embroidered cushions. "Now don't tell me you met at the clinic?"

"No, actually we have mutual friends," he said, reciting the story Olivia had coached him on for the last seven days. "We met through them."

"Is that a fact?" Sherry exclaimed, patting the cushion next to her. "So Olivia doesn't spend *all* her time delivering babies I take it?"

"Not all of it," Lucas said, turning as Olivia came up behind them. "Which is something I'm very grateful for."

"I say, Olivia," Sherry said in a rigid voice, her icy-blue gaze moving from one, to the other. "It would certainly appear you are one lucky woman."

"Oh, I don't know," Lucas interjected, slipping an arm around Olivia's waist as she joined him. "I tend to believe I'm the lucky one."

"Yes well, isn't that just too precious?" Sherry said, settling back against the cushions, her smile turning brittle. "So tell me where you two lovebirds spent your honeymoon."

"We haven't had much of a chance to take one yet, but..." He stopped, pulling Olivia close and gazing down at her. "We're working on it, aren't we?"

"Yes," Olivia said, taking a deep breath. "You know, Sherry, we could talk about all this later."

"Have you ever considered a cruise?" Sherry continued, ignoring Olivia and directing her question to Lucas. "They can be wildly romantic. You should let me arrange something."

Lucas looked up at her. "Maybe sometime."

"Well, Olivia," Sherry sighed, stretching her arms out and resting them along the back of the sofa. "A career, now a husband. What's next on the agenda? The pitter-patter of little feet?"

"One thing at a time," Olivia answered in a stiff voice, but Lucas felt her entire body go rigid.

"Oh, come on you two, don't tell me you haven't thought about it. How does that go—first comes love, then come marriage, then comes—"

"Whoa, slow down," Lucas said, glancing up and stopping her with wave of his hand. "We're barely used to married life." He glanced back down at Olivia, giving her a little squeeze. "Right?"

"Right," Olivia said, shifting her gaze to Sherry. "We're in no hurry."

"Okay, okay," Sherry conceded with a shrug, shifting her attention to Olivia and scooting to one side of the sofa. "But sit down and tell me all about how you two met. So you had mutual friends, is that right?"

Lucas stepped to one side as Olivia sat down on the sofa next to Sherry and the two women began talking. Olivia looked in perfect control now— strong, determined and confident as she talked with her cousin about a courtship that had never happened.

"Why, Lucas, I think you positively swept this dear girl right off her feet," Sherry said with a dramatic sigh, sinking back against the cushions. She looked up at him and gave him a conspiratorial wink. "And just between you and me, this wife of yours positively glows whenever she mentions your name. I don't believe I've seen Olivia this starry-eyed since—"

But Sherry's words were drowned out as Grace came bustling through the living room like a whirlwind, clapping and gathering up everyone in her path.

"There will be plenty of time later for catching up," she announced in a loud voice. "Right now we've got a wedding to put together and we've all got things we need to do." Coming to a stop in the middle of the room, she began pointing and shouting out orders. "Monica, you get on the telephone and call Peter. Find out if he and his parents have left yet. The wedding coordinator is on her way and she's going to want input from all of us. Kathleen, you need to get started on that dried flower arrangement and Maury, Kathleen said you wouldn't mind helping Jacob with that load of folding chairs that were delivered this morning. Lucas, Olivia." She pivoted in place, pointing in their direction. "You two need to run back upstairs and finish changing—wool slacks and blazers are way too warm for this weather and you'll want to be comfortable. Sherry, maybe you could give your Aunt Kathleen a hand and Kevin and Joseph, you boys help your father and Uncle Jacob and..."

Her words trailed off as she flung open the French doors leading to the red-bricked patio outside and sailed out across the lawn, catching sight of Sam working on one of the hedges and shouting out some instructions to him.

"Well, we've all been given our orders," Jacob said in a weary voice, lifting himself out of an easy chair and motioning to his brother-in-law. "Come on, Maury, you know how she gets if we don't do what she says."

Lucas laughed as they dutifully marched past, grumbling and grousing, then turned to Olivia. "Maybe we should get changed?"

"You heard the drill sergeant," Olivia mumbled dryly as she rose to her feet. "Sherry, we'll no doubt be seeing you later."

"You can count on it," Sherry assured her as she pushed herself up from the cushions and over to Lucas. Slipping her arm through his again, she looked up at him and smiled. "Olivia knows I'm not one to miss an opportunity to spend a little quality time with the family."

"Quality time with the family," Olivia muttered as she stomped up the stairs and headed towards her bedroom. The words burned in her brain and she felt the fury building in her like steam collecting in a boiler.

"You say something?"

She glanced back at Lucas as he followed her up the stairs and shook her head. "No."

"Sure?"

"Yes, I'm sure," she snapped. She thought of how he'd let Sherry drag him around by the arm and got angry all over again. Men were such idiots. Couldn't he see through all that phony fawning and flattery? "I was just talking to myself."

She reached the top of the steps and turned down the hall towards her room.

"You seem upset," he said as he rounded the corner behind her.

"Do I?" She shrugged casually, but she could hear the anger in her own voice. "I'm not."

He gave her a careful look. "You sure?"

"I think I am capable of knowing how I feel," she said pointedly. "And I feel just fine."

She pushed the door of the bedroom open and stormed inside, but spotting her old, familiar double bed, she skittered to an abrupt halt. She might have told him she was feeling fine, but at the moment she was having a difficult time resisting the urge to fling herself across the bed, just as she had countless times as a kid, and cry her eyes out.

What was the matter with her? Why was she feeling so awful and why was she striking out at him. She was acting like a jealous wife, which was ridiculous since she wasn't one. Still, watching Sherry with Lucas just now had made her furious, bringing back a freight car full of memories and dredging up old insecurities she buried long ago.

For as far back as she could remember, it seemed as though Sherry had gone after whatever it was she had—not because Sherry particularly wanted it. Sherry had just been intent on making sure that she didn't have it. It hadn't mattered if it had been a toy, a book, a car, a job, or even the captain of the San Marcos High School football team—if Olivia had wanted it, Sherry had wanted to take it away. It had been Sherry who had told her with such relish the truth about Charles, Sherry who had seduced him in order to drive home the point of his lies and infidelity, but all that had been years ago.

Olivia remembered the long talks she'd had with her mother over the years about Sherry, how Grace had explained about Sherry's troubled childhood, about her loneliness and her pain over her mother's rejection. Olivia had sympathy, but it hadn't made dealing with the constant competition any easier.

But she wasn't the same little girl she'd once been, she was no longer bothered by Sherry's incessant bragging and vicious rivalry—so why in the world was she allowing it to bother her now?

"Look, if you'd like some privacy, I could go downstairs for a while."

"Whatever you want," she said with a forced casualness, reaching for her suitcase from the closet and tossing it down on the bed.

"I just thought...." He stopped, giving his head a shake. "You just seem a little upset about something. If I've done something—"

"You haven't done anything," she insisted, cutting him off. "And I'm not upset." She pulled out a pair of soft denim jeans and a polo shirt. "But if you'd like to go downstairs for a while longer, it's fine with me." She snatched up the clothes and stalked across the room towards the small bathroom. "And who knows, maybe if you hurry you can catch Sherry. I'm sure she'd be happy to keep you company. After all, there's nothing she likes better than spending *quality* time with her family."

She stepped into the bathroom and slammed the door behind her. Walking to the sink, she looked at herself in the mirror. The woman looking back at her was a stranger.

"What are you doing?" she demanded of the image in the mirror. "Are you out of your mind?"

Suddenly the emotions of the last several months, of losing Rachel and Ted, of coming to terms with raising their child alone, of Monica's marriage and seeing all of her family again, engulfed her and she burst into tears. What was happening to her? This wasn't her. She was behaving completely irrationally, completely out of character for herself and it had to stop.

"It has to stop right now," she mumbled to the image staring back at her in the mirror and looking more familiar now. "You've got to pull yourself together, think about your condition, think about the ba—"

The baby. Like a light coming on in a dark room, suddenly everything had become clear. The baby. There wasn't anything the matter with her. She was simply going to have a baby. Her hormones were running wild, causing mood swings as dramatic and as debilitating as any she'd counseled her patients on.

How smug she must have been, sitting behind her desk and instructing patient after patient on the dramatic changes in their moods, calmly assuring them not to worry, that what they were feeling was completely normal and would surely pass in time—all words that were true, but did little to actually make them feel better. She understood now, realized just how powerful those mood swings could be, and how stressful it was.

She glanced down at the clothes in her arms, thinking about how she had snatched them up and stalked past Lucas with such drama, such righteous indignation. Good Lord, he must think she was an idiot—she'd certainly acted like one.

"And those stupid things I said," she groaned to that old, familiar image in the mirror looking back at her. "What must he think?"

The last thing she felt like doing was facing him again, but she had to go out there and apologize. Tossing her jeans and shirt on to the small counter by the sink, she slipped out of her wool skirt and jacket. If only she could hide in the bathroom for the rest of the afternoon.

She stepped into her jeans, thinking about what a fool she had made of herself. She must have sounded like a shrew—a jealous shrew. What kind of explanation could she offer, what kind of excuse could she make?

"What is the matter with this?" she muttered, when the zipper of her jeans stopped and pinched. The last thing she needed right now was a broken zipper.

But when she looked down, she realized to her dismay that it wasn't the zipper that was causing the problem.

"Oh no," she groaned, sucking her small, protruding tummy in tight. She may only be twelve weeks along, but already her waistline had expanded.

"Olivia?"

She jumped at the sound of Lucas's voice on the other side of the door. Fumbling with the zipper, she managed to pull it closed, but the jeans felt tight and uncomfortable. Dropping her shirt down over the front of her jeans, she gave herself an objective glance in the mirror. She didn't look pregnant yet—did she?

"The coast is clear, if that's what you're waiting for," he said, his soft voice barely audible through the door. "I'm through changing."

Olivia felt every muscle in her body go rigid. As much as she dreaded facing him, the longer she stayed hidden away, the more foolish she felt. Resigned if not determined, she reached for the door. However before she could turn the knob, her courage deserted her. What was she going to say, what excuse could she give him to explain why she'd behaved like a lunatic? He'd been so wonderful since they'd gotten there, had been so adept at winning over Monica and her parents as well as the rest of her family. He'd been so convincing as her husband he almost had her believing they were married too.

"Olivia? Are you okay?"

The quiet tap on the door had been so unexpected, she jumped again.

"Olivia, can you hear me?"

"Y-yes, I can hear you. I'm fine."

"Then open the door."

She took a deep breath, feeling the constraints of the denim tight against her waist and trying her best to ignore it. She couldn't think about that now. What she had to concentrate on was finding the courage to open the door and face the man standing on the other side.

Turning the knob, she slowly pulled the door open, giving her tummy one last quick glance in the mirror. She felt overstuffed but hopefully she didn't look that way. When she opened the door, she found herself looking up into his coal-black eyes.

"Hi."

"Hi," he said, his voice sounding concerned. "I was getting worried about you."

"Were you?"

"Yes, I was. You seemed so upset."

He looked so completely bewildered she felt emotion swell thick in her throat. She wasn't sure at that moment if she felt like bursting into tears again, or hugging him. Except her emotions had gotten her into enough trouble for one day and she had to be careful not to let it happen again. She'd overreacted at seeing Sherry earlier and it would be easy to over-react with him right now too. If she was ever going to get through this, she was going to have to start thinking more like a doctor and less like a mother-to-be.

"Oh, Lucas, I'm sorry."

Chapter Five

"Anyway, this whole thing has just been more difficult than I'd anticipated. As you can probably see, I'm not very comfortable being dishonest with everyone and it's just got my emotions going haywire," Olivia concluded with a heavy sigh. "Not to mention the whole emotional thing with my sister getting married and seeing everyone again." She turned back from the window, clutching her hands nervously in front of her. "And I wasn't really snapping at you—well, I was snapping *at* you but it wasn't because I was angry at you or anything only—"

"Olivia," Lucas said in a quiet voice, interrupting her. "Stop." He slowly made his way across the room towards her. "You don't owe me any explanation."

"Well, I feel as though I do," she said, glancing

down at her hands. "I behaved badly and you didn't deserve it. I'm sorry."

"You've done nothing to apologize for," he insisted, reaching out and placing a hand on her upper arm.

He'd been touching her all morning—holding her hand, putting his arm around her, pulling her close. But that had been because he'd been pretending to be her husband, all part of their "act" for the benefit of the others. Except no one was watching them now. It was just the two of them now, alone in the bedroom of her childhood, making the touch feel more familiar, more intimate.

"Nevertheless, I'd like to anyway," she said, looking up at him. "And I'd told you before Sherry and I...well, there's some history there." Purposely, she moved to one side, stepping past him. "It was all pretty sophomoric and juvenile and happened a very long time ago." Stopping, she turned back around, lifting her gaze to his. "And I don't have a clue as to why I'd let it bother me this afternoon other than to say the emotions of the day just caught up with me. I'm sorry I was short with you and I hope you'll accept my apology."

He regarded her for a long moment, so long in fact she grew uncomfortable. Didn't he believe her? That really would have been ironic, considering the whoppers she'd been telling all day.

"On one condition," he said finally.

"One condition?" She swallowed hard, her throat feeling dry and raw. "What's that?"

"You stop apologizing to me about everything and try and relax just a little." He slowly started across the room towards her. "Your sister is getting married for heaven's sake. Relax and enjoy it."

She hadn't realized until that moment she'd been holding her breath because she let it out now in one long sigh. He was absolutely right. Her incessant worrying wasn't going to help anything, and really wasn't good for her, given her condition.

With good-natured drama, she offered him her hand as he approached. "You've just got yourself a deal."

Lucas laughed, taking her hand in his and giving it a shake. "So okay, you think maybe we should be getting downstairs?" With her hand in his, he started to pull her towards the door. "We did, after all, receive our orders."

"My mother," Olivia laughed, letting him lead her out into the hall. "She does have a way of putting things, doesn't she? I think she was a drill sergeant in another life."

"Hey, the important thing is she can get things done," he pointed out. "That's the kind of person I like working for me."

"Oh?" she asked as they rounded the corner at the top of the stairs. "And just what is it you hired her for?"

He dropped her hand suddenly. "I only meant that...I just meant she's the kind of person I'd want on my side." He descended several steps ahead of her. "Did I happen to mention you look great in jeans?"

"Uh...thank-you," she stammered, the unexpected compliment taking her by surprise. She was suddenly very aware of the unnatural tightness of the denim around her waist and ran her hand self-consciously across her tummy. "Your's look good on you too."

And they did. Somewhere in the midst of her emotional outburst and embarrassment, she'd managed to take notice.

"Well, come on," he said, grabbing her hand again and giving it a tug. "We've probably kept everyone waiting long enough."

"Well aren't you two just as cute as you can be?"

They both turned at the sound of Sherry's voice as they passed by the kitchen on their way to the backyard.

"Sherry, you're still here," Olivia said, making a point to sound friendly and cheerful.

"Still here and don't you two look just adorable dressed alike in your blue jeans." She moved a manicured finger back and forth. "His and hers, how cute."

Olivia and Lucas both came to a stop and stared at one another.

"She's right," Olivia observed with a gasp. In a polo shirt and jeans, she looked like a scaled down version of him. Their pale yellow shirts were not only the same color, they were virtually identical—right down to the same "polo player" logo embroidered on the front. She looked up at him. "Maybe I should run up and change."

"No, you look great," he said, tugging at her arm as she started to turn around. "Besides, you heard Sherry." His smile broadened as he gave her hand a squeeze. "We're adorable—cute! And personally I think you have great taste in clothes."

* * *

"Of course, Maury's going to tell you he has never used a wood on that course," Jacob mumbled, as he pulled a small metal tamper from his pocket and gently patted down the smoldering tobacco in the bowl of a carved, Meerschaum pipe. "But his game reflects it too. He can drive the ball, I'll give him that, but he can't putt worth a dime. And you know what they say—drive for show, putt for dough." He walked over to the beveled glass cabinet built into the paneled wall of the den and pulled out the crystal decanter of brandy. "And just between you and me, he's not nearly as good as he thinks he is."

Jacob lifted the decanter, starting to pour more of the amber liquid into Lucas's glass, but stopped when Lucas waved him off.

"No more for me, sir, thank you," Lucas said, lifting his glass and finishing the last swallow. The brandy was excellent, feeling warm and soothing as it made its way down, but he'd had too much already. His first day as a member of the Martin family had been a hectic one and what he needed was about ten hours sleep to recuperate. He just wasn't sure how much rest he'd be getting tonight. "And I think it's probably time for me to turn in."

"What's this 'sir' business," Jacob scolded, pouring himself another glass. "I'm Dad and don't you forget it." He turned and looked at the grandfather clock in the corner. "And you're right, it is getting late. You'd better get on upstairs. Heaven knows I don't want to get that wife of yours upset. She's got one heck of a temper when she gets all riled up, although I'm sure you already know all about that.''

Lucas nodded as he lifted himself off the comfortable wing-backed chair. The news came as no surprise to him. She'd been pretty riled up this morning, although he wouldn't exactly have classified that as anger. She'd been more emotional, more upset than angry, but he was hardly one to judge. There was a lot he didn't know about the woman.

''Well, good night, sir—uh, I mean...Dad,'' he corrected, feeling awkward with the lie.

''Good night, my boy,'' Jacob said, swirling the last of his brandy around in his glass. ''And don't you let my daughter give you any grief about that one o'clock tee time. You tell her it was all my doing, okay?''

''I'll tell her to come talk to you if she has a problem with it,'' he said as he started out the door.

''Oh, uh, now, uh, I don't think you should be doing that,'' Jacob stammered.

''Good night,'' Lucas said with a laugh, quickly slipping out of the door and down the hall before Jacob had a chance to protest.

The house had been a virtual hotbed of sound and activity for most of the day, but it was quiet now—so quiet in fact that even his footsteps along the carpet made a sound. He'd never had ''in-laws'' when he'd been married to Pam, never had any cousins to meet, any aunts and uncles to try and keep straight. With her mother gone and never having known her father, Pam had been pretty much alone in the world. At the time he hadn't thought much about it, but he was beginning to understand how nice it could be to marry into a family, how comforting it could feel to be greeted and accepted. Of course this was all a pretense—he knew it, Olivia knew it. But to the Martins, he was their son-in-law. He liked Jacob, whose grousing about being henpecked and picked on by the women in his life did little to hide his adoration of them. He liked Grace and her drill sergeant maternalism that was always tempered by her love for her family. Actually he found everyone he'd met to be pleasant and friendly. Olivia Martin's family were warm and generous people and he found himself feeling almost remorseful about not being truthful with them.

Olivia. He thought of his "wife" upstairs in the bedroom they were sharing and his stomach tightened into a hard, round knot. The day had been an exhausting one. After they had joined the family to meet with the wedding coordinator, they'd been whisked away for a battery of appointments. Olivia had gone with her mother and sister to be fitted for the dress she'd wear as maid of honor while he had gone with Maury and the boys to be measured and sized for tuxedos. Then there had been a buffet supper and a succession of even more family and scores of friends to meet, followed by an evening dessert at the home of Monica's soon-to-be in-laws. He was exhausted and felt as though he could sleep for a week, but he doubted he would be getting any rest tonight—despite the fatigue.

The words he had used to allay her regret about their sleeping arrangements had been sincere, but at ten o'clock in the morning being "adult" about things had been easy. Now, with the long night stretching out in front of him, the situation didn't seem nearly as reasonable. Maybe they were both adults and maybe they could share a room and still respect each other's space, but that didn't mean it wouldn't be awkward.

He'd spent the day immersed in the world of Olivia Martin—the world of her childhood, of her family and of the young woman she once had been and he was ready for a breather. It wasn't that he didn't like what he had learned about the woman— but that was the problem. He was liking it *too* much. The more time he spent with Olivia, the more he found himself liking her. Playing the part of her husband was easy—maybe too easy and that was dangerous. What he would give for a cold, impersonal hotel room to collapse into and a strong dose of reality.

He reached the top of the stairs and turned down the hall towards the bedroom. Unfortunately Olivia's bedroom was anything but cold and impersonal and he would be having no break from the woman tonight.

She had gone up to bed nearly an hour earlier, looking drained and exhausted. With any luck, she would be asleep, at least that's what he hoped. Not only would it make things less awkward, but she really had looked as though she could use some rest. The day had no doubt been emotionally draining for her.

At the bedroom door he stopped, suddenly unsure. Was he supposed to knock, or just barge in? What if she were changing, or just getting out of the shower. He didn't want to embarrass her, or himself, but if she was already asleep, he didn't want to risk waking her up by knocking either.

"Olivia?"

He'd barely whispered, but in the quiet hallway his voice had penetrated the silence as shrilly as a shout. He waited for what seemed like an eternity to his tired mind and exhausted body, yet he could hear nothing from inside the room.

Lifting a hand, he rapped the knuckle of one finger against the wood gently. "Olivia?"

He was just about to knock again when he heard Jacob coming up the stairs. Since it would be difficult to explain to his father-in-law why he was knocking on the door of his own bedroom, he reached for the doorknob, giving it a quick turn. Wrenching the door open, he quickly stepped inside.

"You startled me."

He stared at Olivia from across the bedroom, feeling a little like a cat burglar who'd just been surprised by the lady of the house. She was sitting up in the bed leaning against the headboard, a book propped up on her lap, her hair tied in a ponytail and glasses perched on the end of her nose. The robe she wore covered her from chin to ankle—even her feet were covered up with thick, furry slippers.

Why couldn't she have been wearing some slinky nightgown, some thin, little lacy teddy? Why couldn't she display the kind of obvious sensuality her cousin Sherry did, the kind that came up and hit a man in the face like a ton of bricks? He understood that kind of attempt on a woman's part and could resist it. But this smoldering wholesomeness, this little-girl-lost appeal and subtle but unmistakable charm was a killer. It could bypass his safeguards and breach all his precautions. The woman was dangerous, there was no doubt about it, and the night was going to be very, very long.

"I—uh, I knocked," he stammered. For some reason he found himself pointing and gesturing in a manner that was totally out of character for him. "But I heard Jacob—uh, I mean your father and I—uh, I thought—uh, well, I thought—"

"Lucas," she said in a quiet voice, cutting him off. "Relax, it's all right. It's your room too."

"I, uh, I thought you'd be asleep."

She slipped her glasses off her nose. "I thought I would be too," she said, leaning over to set them on the nightstand beside the bed. "I'm exhausted but I can't seem to settle down." She sat back up, lifting the book from her lap. "I thought maybe reading would make me sleepy."

"Doesn't look like it's worked too well."

She tossed the book down on the bed beside her and shook her head. "It hasn't."

He drew in a deep breath, suddenly unsure as to what to do with his hands. "Maybe I need a book."

"You okay?"

"Oh, sure, just…restless." He started towards the bathroom, then stopped. Shaking his head, he let his hands drop to his side. "Look, don't pay any attention to me. It's just a little…"

"Awkward?" she said, finishing for him when his words drifted off.

He gave her a helpless look. "More than I thought it would be."

She nodded in agreement. "I know, I'm sorry. I

shouldn't have let my mother talk us out of going to a hotel.''

He waved off her concern, but the gesture was an easy, natural one for him this time. ''Don't talk crazy. And what was our agreement about you apologizing?''

She laughed this time. ''Okay, okay. No more apologizing.'' She closed her book. ''But you just might live to regret that someday.''

''I'll take my chances,'' he said, pushing himself away from the door and heading for the closet. ''Okay, so now that we're being so adult about all this, where do you want me to make my bed?''

''Oh, no,'' Olivia said, shaking her head emphatically. ''Since we are adults we can be fair.'' She sat up, swinging her feet to the floor. Pulling open a drawer on the nightstand, she pulled out a coin, holding it up for him to see. ''Here's a quarter, I'll flip you for the bed.''

It was his turn to shake his head, which he did, even more emphatically. ''No dice, Doc. You're taking the bed.'' He quickly raised a hand, stopping her when she started to protest. ''I insist!'' He turned and started for the closet. ''There are a bunch of blankets up here.'' He opened the doors, pulling items off a high shelf. ''Plenty to make a comfy bed right here on the floor.''

''Lucas,'' she said, rising to her feet. ''I wouldn't feel right. You've been inconvenienced enough already.''

''Then don't inconvenience me any more by arguing,'' he warned, tossing a stack of blankets and pillows on to the carpet and putting his hands on his hips. "Now get back into bed. You should have been asleep an hour ago."

She was smiling when she looked up at him, and he felt a sudden tightness in his chest. How did she do that? How could she get to him like that, make him forget he had to be careful. It was what made her so dangerous, what made it so important that he be on his guard. She could get him talking and before long he'd find himself poking fun and teasing her. But while their joking and teasing might have helped ease the awkwardness between them, he felt anything but relaxed when she looked at him. There was something in her eyes, something that made him realize sleeping arrangements had little to do with what was really making him awkward. Where he was in proximity to her made little difference. The truth was, he'd become aware of her in a way he hadn't been aware of a woman in a very long time and it wouldn't matter if she were in the next bed or in the next room—the awareness was there and it was dangerous.

"You always this bossy?" she asked.

"Pretty much."

"Hmm," she mused, bending down and picking up a fluffy down comforter from the stack of bedding he'd removed from the closet. "The way you order people around you'd think you were the doctor."

"Oh, no," he said, grabbing one end of the comforter she held and helping spread it out on the carpet. "I wouldn't have made a good doctor, not like you."

She reached for several of the blankets, looking

up and smiling at him again. "And what makes you think I'm good? Maybe I'm a quack?"

"You? A quack?" He shook his head, helping her stack the blankets over the top of the comforter. "Naw. I hear what the nurses and the orderlies and office staff say about you."

She arched an eyebrow. "They talk about me?"

"Sure, all the time."

"Oh, really?" She frowned and reached for a pillow. "What do they say?"

"The women all say if they were having a baby, they'd want you to deliver it."

"Really?" She tossed him the pillow and reached for another one.

"Yeah," he said, catching the pillow and tossing it on to his makeshift bed.

"And the men?" she asked, winding up to throw the second pillow.

He held up his hands, preparing for the catch. "Same thing."

She lowered the pillow. "They want me to deliver them?"

He rolled his eyes. "Their wives, girlfriends, you know what I mean."

She considered this for a moment, then shrugged. "Well, I guess that's good."

"Sure and they also say—" He stopped abruptly and shook his head. "No, I better not. I wouldn't want to make you self-conscious or get anyone in trouble."

"What? You can't stop now?"

He gave her an innocent look. "I can."

"No you can't. I have a right to know what my co-workers are saying about me, don't I?"

"I don't know, do you?"

"Of course I do. If there is a problem with a co-worker, I think I should know about it."

"Co-workers," he corrected. "More than one."

"More than one?" Her eyes opened wide in surprise. "Then all the more reason I should know."

"But I wouldn't want to be responsible for getting anyone into trouble."

"No one is going to get into trouble."

"Promise?"

"Lucas! I demand that you tell me."

He couldn't hold back any longer, his mouth breaking into a full grin. Her eyes were full of indignation and she'd all but stamped her foot. She didn't look too much like cool, professional Dr. Olivia Martin now. She looked like Jacob and Grace Martin's fiery tempered daughter—and he was finding he liked teasing her maybe a little too much.

"You're too easy, Doc," he said, no longer able to keep the laughter back. "Relax, you've got nothing to worry about. Your male co-workers all think very highly of you."

She eyed him suspiciously. "You're not just saying that?"

"No, no" he assured her, her stern look making him laugh even harder. "Of course not. In fact, they all think you're a fox."

She blinked. "A...fox?"

"Yeah, a fox."

She regarded him for a moment as he worked on his bed, as if trying to decide if he were pulling her leg or not, then reacted. Raising a pillow over her head, she hurled it towards him.

"That's for being such a wise guy," she said as the pillow caught him full in the face. "And here I was going to tell you what all the nurses had to say about you." With a smug grin, she turned and started towards her bed. "But gosh, I don't want to make you self-conscious either."

She'd only taken a few steps when a pillow caught her in the back of the head.

"Oops, sorry, Doc," he said, seeing beyond her stern expression to the humor in her eyes. He was beginning to think he might not be the only one who enjoyed the teasing between them. Smiling, he gave her his best innocent look and helpless little shrug. "Slipped."

"Oh dear," she sighed, bending down and picking up the pillow with a dramatic swipe of her hand. "I'm afraid you've asked for it now."

"Oh my, I'd say somebody got up on the wrong side of the bed."

Olivia glared first at her father and then at Monica, who sat in a chair across the breakfast table from him. The aroma of freshly brewed coffee swirled around her like a mischievous little cloud, mocking her with what she knew she couldn't have. She didn't doubt she looked a little harried in her ratty, old terry robe, with her hair falling down her shoulders in a tangled mess, but they didn't have to enjoy it so much.

"There is no right or wrong side of a bed," she humorlessly informed them, squinting from the light of the sunny breakfast nook. Her head ached and she was fairly confident that every muscle in her body ached. Despite eight solid hours of sleep, she'd woke up this morning feeling more exhausted than she had the night before. Shuffling to the table, she stopped at her father's chair, leaning down to give him a peck on the cheek. "It's a proven medical fact."

"Well, that's a relief," Jacob acknowledged with a nod, adjusting his morning newspaper just enough to allow for the kiss. "Otherwise I would have had to conclude you'd gotten up on it."

"Oh, Professor Martin, you and your deductive reasoning," she sighed, giving his shoulder a pat. She rounded the table, sliding into the chair alongside her sister. The sarcasm in her voice was manufactured, the grumpiness was not. "Your students must love you in the morning."

"Well, we could always discuss bedside manner, Dr. Martin, if you'd prefer," Jacob suggested dryly, peering at her from over the top of his newspaper.

"Okay, okay," she conceded good-naturedly. "Maybe we're all not so chipper in the mornings."

"Well, I'm not surprised," Monica said, reaching for the coffee carafe from its wooden trivet on the table to pour her sister a cup. "Considering the racket I heard coming from your bedroom last night." She stopped when Olivia waved off the offer of a cup. "What? You're refusing a cup of coffee?" She gave her head a small shake as she returned the carafe to its holder. "I never thought I'd see the day."

"Very funny," Olivia said, brushing off her sister's comment with a careless wave of the hand. She couldn't let herself overreact the way she had with Sherry. "Maybe if you didn't drink so much coffee you wouldn't be up late listening to all those bumps in the night."

"Oh this was more than a bump in the night," Monica claimed breezily. "It was quite a commotion I'd say."

Jacob peered from over the top of his newspaper. "I'm not sure this is something I want to hear about."

"I'm talking about a pillow fight, Daddy," Monica laughed, crumbling her paper napkin and tossing it towards him. "I still recognize the sounds of one when I hear it."

"Pillow fight?" He lifted the newspaper just high enough to deflect the napkin, then turned an arched brow to Olivia. "You and Lucas had a pillow fight?"

Olivia leaned forward, putting her elbows on the table and resting her chin on her hand. She thought of Lucas's surprised expression when she'd caught him in the face with the pillow, and smiled. The few swipes they'd taken at each other hardly qualified as a pillow fight, but they'd helped ease the awkwardness between them—at least for a while.

"There are some things you never lose your touch for," she said to Monica, playing along.

"My daughter the doctor," Jacob muttered, giving his head a shake as he turned his attention back to his newspaper.

"Who started it?"

Olivia's gaze slid to her sister.

Monica laughed. "Just what I thought." She picked up her own coffee cup and raised it to her lips. "Poor Lucas, we really should have a talk. There are some things I think I should warn him about."

"Let me remind you, little sister, blood is thicker than water."

Olivia watched as Monica took a drink of coffee. Between med-school and living in Seattle, coffee had become a primary staple of her diet and a day hadn't passed in the last twelve weeks when she hadn't wanted a cup. Which was why, as she watched Monica taking a sip just now, she found herself feeling very strange. The aroma, which had smelled so wonderfully inviting only a moment before, suddenly became insufferable, closing in on her like a toxic substance, suffocating her.

"I don't know if there's a diplomatic way of saying this," Monica said, watching Olivia closely. "But, big sister, you don't look so good. Are you feeling all right?"

"Fine," Olivia insisted, her heart beating like thunder in her ears. "I'm fine."

Monica's gaze narrowed and the smile faded from her lips. "You sure?"

Olivia drew in a deep breath, swallowing hard. The peculiar sensation that had struck so suddenly, disappeared just as abruptly.

"Of course I'm sure," she said, sitting back in the chair. She was pleased with the cool, controlled tone of her voice—her doctor's voice, the one she used when it was important to keep emotion out of what she was saying and this definitely was one of those times.

"You know, now that I look at you, you do look a little peaked," Jacob observed, lowering his paper and taking off his reading glasses. "Maybe you're coming down with something."

"I'm not coming down with something," she insisted with a silly laugh.

"Well, you never can be sure about those things," her father advised in a sage voice. "And everyone knows the worst place for germs is in a doctor's office."

"That's just an old wives' tale," Olivia snorted with a dismissive wave of her hand.

"But it's a well-known fact that doctors make the worst kind of patients," Monica chipped in.

"A well-known fact," Olivia repeated with a mutter, giving her sister a skeptical look. "Sounds very scientific."

Jacob set down his paper. "Do you have a fever?"

"No," Olivia said with a humorless laugh. "I don't have a fever and I'm not sick." Olivia leaned back in her seat. "And if you two don't stop picking on me, I'm going back to bed."

"Who's picking on you?"

They all looked up as Grace sailed into the breakfast nook, slipping the bib of her apron over her head. Olivia didn't think she'd ever been quite so relieved to see her mother as she was at that moment.

"They're ganging up on me," she complained as her mother leaned down and gave her a hug. "I don't brush my hair one morning, and they're making a federal case out of it.''

Grace straightened up, giving Monica and Jacob a questioning look. "You two being mean to this poor child?''

"I was just pointing out to the good doctor that she looked like she might be coming down with something,'' Monica pointed out.

Grace's eyes opened wide and she took a step back. "You're sick?''

"I am *not* sick,'' Olivia asserted with a frustrated sigh.

"No fever,'' Grace announced, running a hand along Olivia's cheek.

"I'm just a little tired, that's all.'' Olivia reached for her mother's hand and gently guided it away from her cheek.

"Of course that could be from staying up all night having pillow fights,'' Monica added.

Grace gave her a skeptical look. "What's this about a pillow fight?''

"Nothing about a pillow fight,'' Olivia maintained. "And there is no fever, no sniffles—nothing. I'm fine.''

Grace reached out, putting a hand on Olivia's chin and making a play of inspecting her closely. "Personally I'd say those two don't know what they're talking about. You look great to me.'' She leaned close, her eyes narrowing with scrunity. "Glowing even.''

"Uh-oh, glowing. You know what that means,'' Monica warned, raising a brow. "Is there anything we should know? Any announcement you'd like to make?''

Olivia's smile stiffened and she felt an icy chill move down her spine but she forced herself not to react. Monica had obviously been teasing and had no idea whatsoever just how close she'd come to guessing the truth.

"You always were my favorite," she said in a dry tone, shooting first Monica a cool look, and then her father. "You know that don't you?"

Grace laughed, giving Olivia's cheek a pat. "Now if that isn't a hint to get breakfast started, I don't know what is." She straightened up and turned into the kitchen, pulling down pans from the rack above the stove. "A good breakfast is going to make everyone feel better."

"Look who we found wandering the hallway," Kathleen announced as she and Maury walked into the kitchen with Lucas in tow. "I think you've got yourself one hungry son-in-law, Gracie."

Olivia turned around, her gaze catching Lucas's. Suddenly she was aware of her ratty robe and snarly hair in a whole new light. He'd still been asleep when she'd stumbled out of bed and she had to admit that hadn't exactly been by accident. Last night had been difficult enough. The pillow fight had broken the tension between them for a while, but things had become uncomfortable after that. They'd given each other as much privacy as possible, had taken turns in the bathroom, exchanged polite conversation and bid each other a pleasant good-night but the tension had been there—thick and heavy. It had only been because of her years of conditioning in med-school, where she'd been forced to learn to fall asleep anytime and anywhere, that she'd gotten any sleep at all. But at least last night there had been the darkness to cloak them, easing the awkwardness a little. She hadn't been ready to deal with it in the stark light of day, which is why she'd forced herself up and out of bed before he'd woken up.

"Good morning, everyone," Lucas said, raising a hand in greeting to the others in the room. His gaze came to rest on Olivia, and he smiled. "Good morning."

"Oh go on, don't be embarrassed," Kathleen said, prodding him with a little push on the shoulder. "It's perfectly acceptable for a husband to give his wife a good morning kiss."

It was probably just as well that her Aunt Kathleen was out of arm's reach, because Olivia would have liked to have strangled her at that moment. How she wished she could open her eyes and start the day all over again, because this one was becoming more and more like a bad dream. Worst of all, Lucas looked every bit as embarrassed as she felt as he started across the room towards her, which only made her feel worse.

"Good morning," he said in a low voice, slipping a hand on her shoulder and placing a small kiss on top of her head.

She looked up at him, wishing she could say how sorry she was. "Good morning."

"All right then," Grace said in her drill sergeant voice. She pulled open the door of the refrigerator and began pulling items from the shelf. "Bacon, sausage and eggs for everyone?"

Chapter Six

Lucas hated to think that the look on Olivia's face was a result of him having to kiss her. His ego had been bruised enough when she hadn't figured out who he was, when she'd failed to put two and two together once he'd told her his last name. While part of him was pleased with the anonymity, he couldn't help wondering if she ever reflected on him at all, if she ever wondered about his past, about where he'd come from and where he was going. Wasn't she even a little bit curious about how he wound up patrolling the corridors of the Mt. Rainier clinic?

But she looked anything but curious now, sitting there staring up at him. If anything, she looked as though she'd just been kissed by a frog—and hadn't cared much for the experience.

He'd heard her when she'd gotten up this morning—not that she'd been noisy. Just the opposite actually. She'd moved so soundlessly back and forth

in front of him he'd had to peek through slitted lids
to make sure she was still in the room. It had been
hard pretending to be asleep—especially given the
fact that he'd been awake for hours, but it just had
seemed easier that way. The night had been a brutal
one for him—strained, tense and endlessly long. He
had lain in the darkness and listened to her low,
steady breathing. The sweet, delicate sound had in-
vaded his brain, seeping into his blood until he
couldn't think of anything else. Images had filled
his mind, images of her eyes, the tilt of her chin, the
sun in her hair and the fullness of her lips. He remembered the softness of her hand, the sound of her
laughter and the fire in her eyes—fire that had come
from anger when her cousin had attempted to flirt
with him. Those sounds and images swirled around
his head, creating a kaleidoscope of sensation that
had turned his blood to fire and his common sense
to mush.

He'd made a big mistake, he knew that now, a
mistake he'd thought he would never make again.
He'd come to the aid of a damsel in distress, only
this time he was the one in need of rescuing. Olivia
Martin had gotten his attention without even trying.
She'd smiled at him and he'd practically melted at
her feet. He might have convinced himself he was
helping her out of a jam by agreeing to come to
Santa Barbara, but he realized now he would have
grasped at any excuse. The woman was getting to
him—she'd done nothing to try and yet she was getting to him. And if he wasn't careful, he was going
to do something stupid like start believing she was
interested in him for something other than playing

the part of her husband. He wasn't her husband, he wasn't even the Lucas McCall that so many other women were impressed by. To her he was just Luke, the kindly security guard who had simply been in the right place at the right time and been willing to help.

Which was why he had let her believe he was asleep. He needed time to think, to gather his strength, to marshal his forces for the new day. He had managed to survive his first day and his first night in the role of Olivia Martin's new husband, but the job hadn't been an easy one. He still had six days and five interminably long nights left to go, and at this moment he wasn't entirely sure how he was going to survive them. The only thing he could do was to try and keep his distance from her when he could and as best he could—and pretending to be asleep this morning had been a start.

"How do you like your eggs, Lucas?" Kathleen asked, opening the pantry door and taking an apron identical to Grace's from a hook inside the door. "Over easy, scrambled or are you an omelette person like me?"

"Omelette, definitely," he said, turning away from Olivia and trying not to think of the strained, uncomfortable look in her eyes. He walked across the kitchen, taking the apron from Kathleen. "And I'll take that." He slipped the strap over his head, smiling at the look of utter surprise on her face as well as everyone else's. "I make a mean one."

"A man who cooks," Grace said with a dramatic swoon, clutching at her heart. "Lucas McCall, I swear, if my daughter hadn't married you, I would have.''

"Make me an offer," Jacob called out to him from the breakfast nook.

Everyone laughed at that, even Olivia, especially when Grace sent a damp dish towel flying in his direction. Working in the kitchen with Grace and Kathleen was a welcome diversion and soon the entire household was awake and ready for breakfast. He kept busy, shredding cheese, dicing onions, cracking eggs and frying bacon until platters of food lined the kitchen counter and everyone crowded around to help themselves. But despite his efforts, his thoughts kept moving back to Olivia, who sat quietly at the table in her robe and slippers. She'd barely looked at him since that peculiar look she had given him after he'd placed that kiss on the top of her head. When she made no move to serve herself some breakfast, he grabbed a plate and filled it with bacon, toast and a big slice of the omelette he'd made.

"Doctors say breakfast is the most important meal of the day," he said, setting the plate down in front of her.

She looked down at the plate and then lifted her gaze up to him. "Yeah, but what do they know?"

He slid into the chair beside hers, reaching for the coffeepot and pouring himself a cup. "Not hungry?"

She looked down at the plate of food. "Actually, I'm not much of a breakfast eater," she said, looking back at him. "But it was sweet of you to bring me some."

"You might want to try it," he urged, picking up a fork from the place mat and putting it into hand. "I wasn't kidding when I said I make a good one."

She smiled up at him, taking the fork from him and spearing a piece of omelette and popping it into her mouth. "You're right. It's delicious." She took another bite. "Most important meal of the day you say?"

He shook his head, picking up his cup and taking a sip. "No, that's what *you're* supposed to say."

She nodded, taking another bite of eggs. "I guess I know more than I thought." She watched as he took another sip of coffee. "You're not having any?"

"I will later," he said with a shrug. "I guess I'm not much of a breakfast eater either."

"McCall. McCall," Maury said thoughtfully, sitting across the table from him with a heaping plate full of food. "Gracie mentioned something about you being in the security business? You wouldn't have anything to do with McCall Security would you?"

Lucas fumbled with the cup in his hand, thrown by Maury's sudden recognition. "Uh, yeah," he stammered, shooting Olivia a quick look. "That's me."

"No fooling," Maury said, obviously impressed. "I thought that name rang a bell. Then that was you I was reading about in *Forbes* a month or two ago?"

"Well there was an article a while back," he said modestly, wondering now if it had been wise to admit to the truth.

"You've done quite well for yourself then, I'm impressed."

"I've been lucky," he said modestly, shooting another glance at Olivia. But she wasn't looking at him. In fact, he didn't think she was even listening to what was going on. She was sitting there staring at the plate of food in front of her.

"Hear that, Jacob?" Maury called out as Jacob headed towards the table with his breakfast plate. "I was reading about your son-in-law."

"Is that so?" Jacob asked, settling into the chair beside Maury. "Not on the wanted posters in the post office I hope."

"Not hardly," Maury said. "In *Forbes* a couple months back. What was it they call him? The new breed of the self-made man?"

"Really?" Jacob turned to Lucas. "Have we got a celebrity in the family?"

"What's this? Lucas a celebrity?" Kathleen asked as she took a seat at the table. "I thought he was a security guard."

"Security guard," Maury scoffed. "He owns the whole dang company."

Kathleen's eyes opened wide as she turned to her sister who was carrying a plate of toasted bagels to the table. "Gracie, why didn't you tell me?"

"Tell you what?" Grace asked innocently. "What are we talking about?"

"Your son-in-law, he's a celebrity."

Lucas squirmed uncomfortably in his chair, wishing now he'd never said anything. In desperation, he turned to Olivia, but looking at her he forgot all about his discomfort. Something was definitely very wrong. She looked terrible, pale and pasty and her lips were strained tight.

"Olivia," he said in a low voice, leaning close. "Olivia, are you all right?" When she looked up at him, her eyes were shimmering and he reacted before he had time to think or to caution himself. Slipping an arm around her shoulders, he pulled her close. "What is? What's the matter?"

She lifted a shaky hand to her lips, shaking her head.

"Are you not feeling well?"

The look in her eyes became even more helpless and she shook her head again.

"Come on," he said, rising to his feet and gently pulling her chair away from the table. "I'll help you upstairs."

"Olivia, sweetheart?" Grace asked, her voice full of concern. "What is it? What's the matter?"

"She's not feeling well," Lucas answered for Olivia, helping her up out of the chair. "I'm just going to help her—"

But before he could get the words out, Olivia bolted from his arms and took off out of the kitchen at a run. Reaction was immediate, with pandemonium breaking out around the breakfast table and everyone talking over everyone else.

"Oh no, I was afraid of this," Monica groaned.

"You know, she didn't look good this morning," Jacob insisted.

"Boy, did she look green, did you see that?" Kevin shouted, jumping to his feet.

"Gnarly," Joseph laughed, popping a sausage into his mouth.

"Quiet everyone. Quiet!" Grace said finally, turning to Lucas. "Go ahead and go. See if she needs anything, then let us know if everything is all right."

He nodded, heading out of the breakfast nook. His heart was racing. It was obvious she hadn't been feeling good, he realized that now. Still, there had been something in the way she had looked at him, something that had left him feeling shaken and uneasy. Of course he told himself he was merely doing his duty in his "role" as her husband going upstairs to check up on her. It had nothing to do with his real concern for her, with him wanting to ride in once again and attempt to rescue her.

At the door of the bedroom he paused, taking a deep breath. The air felt good in his lungs, cleansing and refreshing. Like it or not, he'd made a commitment to the woman and he was duty-bound to abide by it. It wasn't her fault that he was having difficulty keeping his objectivity, that he couldn't seem to stop playing at being her hero even though she'd never asked him to be one.

Turning the doorknob, he walked into the bedroom. Distance and perspective—that's what he had to keep remembering. He had six more days, and he didn't even want to think about the nights. After that, he could go back to his office, back to the boardroom and forget about the good doctor once and for all.

"You okay?"

Olivia looked up. If she'd been concerned how she might look to him earlier, it didn't bother her now. She didn't care that her hair fell in a tangled mess, or that her eyes were watering and her nose was running. She didn't care that she sat on the hard tile floor or that her arms clutched the cold porcelain of the bathroom bowl like it was a life preserver from a sinking ship. She was too distracted, concentrating too hard, too preoccupied thinking *down* when everything—*everything!*—in her system wanted to come up.

She had sailed through those early weeks of her pregnancy, reaching and passing the critical weeks when morning sickness typically occurred. She'd thought she'd been one of the lucky ones, thought she'd safely made it through with no problem, but it was obvious she'd been wrong. And even though she'd studied morning sickness in med-school, had treated numerous patients in her practice, nothing had prepared her for experiencing it firsthand. In the space of a heartbeat, the delicious aroma of eggs and bacon had turned repugnant, causing her entire system to revolt. Never again would she sit and listen to a mother-to-be complain of the horrifying feeling without feeling total and complete empathy.

"No," she croaked, her throat raw and dry.

He took a few hesitant steps farther into the bathroom. "Is there something I can do, something I could get you?"

She shook her head, swatting back a long, tangled lock of hair that fell across her forehead. "Just shoot me."

"Your mother, everybody—" He made a vague gesture with his hands, pointing to some undetermined spot behind him. "Everyone was concerned."

Olivia closed her eyes. She didn't even want to think about that now. "I'm…I'm fine." She pointed to that same undetermined place. "You can tell them I'm fine."

He hesitated for a moment, looking at her as though she were about to erupt at any moment. "Would you like me to…I mean, maybe I should call a doctor."

The concern on his face was real, and as miserable as she was, she found she couldn't help responding. Looking up at him, she shook her head and rolled her eyes. "Oh heavens, not one of them."

Her joking caught him off guard, and he blew out a small laugh. "Yeah, you're right. I forgot." Gingerly, he lowered himself down on to the edge of the tub. "Still feeling pretty bad?"

She drew in a deep breath, trying to ignore the hard knot in her stomach. "I'm not sure yet."

"Do you suppose it could have been something you ate?"

Olivia thought of the fluffy omelette that had been on her plate, she thought of the smell of the bacon frying and the sausages sizzling and her entire body reacted.

"Oh, please," she groaned, everything in her system wanting to reverse itself. "Don't even mention food."

"Okay, okay, sorry, I'm sorry," he said apologetically. "Could I maybe bring you something to sip on—club soda, a mineral water?"

She leaned back, shifting her weight just enough

until the wall supported her back. "That's sweet," she said, the dryness in her mouth making it difficult to speak. "But no, thanks. I don't need anything."

"Hardly sweet," he lamented, looking remorseful. "I figured it was the least I could do given the fact I poisoned you."

She almost felt good enough to laugh—almost. "I told you, it wasn't the breakfast."

"Well, whatever it was, it sure hit you like a freight train."

"Actually, I'm feeling a little better," she said, reaching down to straighten the front of her robe and then attempting to run a hand through her tangled hair. She figured she must be feeling better if she was becoming aware of how she looked.

"I don't know," he mused, regarding her with a critical eye. "You still look a little green around the gills to me."

"I'm okay," she insisted, sitting up straighter and taking another deep breath. "Just a flu bug. Probably a twenty-four hour thing. I'll be fine."

He regarded her for a moment, then reached out his hand. "Come on, you're going back to bed. You don't have to be a doctor to know you don't fool around with a flu bug. You need your rest."

She started to refuse, then thought better of it. She didn't have a flu bug and all the rest in the world wasn't going to make what was wrong with her go away, but a little quiet time away from everyone wouldn't hurt. She didn't relish the thought of facing the questions and concerns she knew would inevitably come and if she was going to tell everyone she had the flu, she might as well act as though she did.

"Bossy, aren't you?" she mumbled as she took his outstretched hand and let him pull her to her feet.

"Oh, lady, you don't know the half of it," he informed her in a wry tone as he placed a hand at her elbow and carefully guided her out of the bathroom and onto the bed. Fluffing the pillow, he waited until she'd laid back, then tucked the blanket around her securely. "Warm enough?"

"This is Santa Barbara," she pointed out. "The place you wear Bermuda shorts all year long?"

He looked down at the blanket and comforter he'd tucked around her and frowned. "I guess it probably wouldn't do to let you get overheated," he said, reaching down and pulling the comforter back. "Is that better?"

It was ridiculous, but watching as he fussed over her had a hard lump of emotion forming in her throat. He looked so concerned as though how she felt really mattered to him. But she had to remind herself she wasn't seeing anything too clearly these days. She couldn't allow herself to trust any of what she was feeling, not with the uproar her body chemistry was in. Hormones were making her feel sentimental now, just the way they had made her feel jealous yesterday and unbelievably nauseous a few moments ago.

"Better, thanks," she whispered, turning away and furiously blinking back the tears that had suddenly welled up in her eyes.

"Sure I can't bring you something?" He lifted a hand, stopping her as she started to answer. "And I promise not to mention—" He stopped and silently mouthed: "F-O-O-D."

She couldn't help laughing. If the truth were known, the killer bout of morning sickness seemed to have ebbed considerably and she wouldn't have minded taking another crack at that delicious omelette. But gobbling down a plateful of breakfast was hardly in keeping with someone suddenly stricken with a flu bug, so she looked up at him and shook her head.

"No thanks."

He hesitated for a moment, then took a few tentative steps backward. "I'll just go downstairs and let the others know you're resting." He turned and walked across the room. At the door, he stopped and turned around. "Let me know if there's anything you want."

"Uh, there is something," she said as he started to open the door.

"What's that?"

"Why didn't you tell me you were Lucas McCall?"

Lucas came to an abrupt halt. "What?"

"Why didn't you tell me you were Lucas McCall?" she repeated.

"Did I miss something here?" He laughed. "I thought I did."

She shook her head. "You told me you were Luke."

He gave his head a confused shake. "But I am Luke."

She scooted up in the bed, shaking her head again. "No you're Lucas McCall—*the* Lucas McCall. Why didn't you tell me?"

"Why would I think you'd know me?" he asked, feeling only a little uncomfortable with the lie. After all, what could he have said? That he had wondered why she hadn't put two and two together, that she hadn't connected his last name with the name of the company, that he'd found it annoying that she didn't know who he really was? If he'd learned anything from his success, it was that modesty was always the best policy. "You don't find that just a little presumptuous?"

"Well I suppose," she admitted. "But you're Lucas McCall for heaven's sake. Everyone in Seattle has heard that name—everyone in the state! I don't think you can pick up a newspaper without reading something about you."

He had to admit his ego had taken a bit of a beating when she hadn't recognized the name earlier, but now he just felt embarrassed. "Well, you know how it is with celebrities," he said in an elaborate voice, once again finding that joking helped him deal with the awkwardness he felt. "The press is always hounding us."

"Oh, *that's* how it is," she said, playing along.

He regarded her for a moment, realizing he was smiling. He appreciated her sense of humor, her sense of the ridiculous.

"Absolutely," he said as he turned and pulled the door open. "Now you get some rest."

"Lucas?"

He stopped and turned back around. "Yes?"

"Why did you...I mean...it's not like you need the money...why did you agree to, you know, help me out?"

That was the question all right—the one he'd been asking himself over and over again. He really didn't have an answer for her—not one that made sense anyway. So stuck for any reasonable explanation he could give her, he simply told her the truth.

"I'm a sucker for a damsel in distress."

Chapter Seven

Lucas let the sugar fall slowly from the teaspoon and into the hot coffee, watching as it disappeared into the murky black depths of the cup. He'd only been up long enough to take a shower and make a quick pot of coffee and yet already he was exhausted. The last three days had been a blur of activity in preparation for Monica's wedding. There had been errands to run, chores to complete and more dinners and luncheons to attend. The way he'd been smiling and shaking hands the last couple of days, he felt like he was running for office. Playing the part of Olivia Martin's husband was turning out to be a more demanding role than he'd anticipated, making him realize that if he had been doing it for the money, he would have earned every cent.

The last few days had been difficult on Olivia as well. Even though she was feeling better, she hadn't been able to shake her flu bug entirely and she'd been forced to curb her activities. While his frayed senses were grateful for a break from the wife who seemed to be consuming his conscious and unconscious mind more and more, the downside was with Olivia incapacitated at times, he'd been stuck with cousin Sherry to contend with.

Olivia's cousin was a woman on a mission, and the last few days he'd had the uncomfortable feeling he'd become her latest target. Sherry had fussed and gushed over him at every opportunity. Normally he would have been flattered by all the attention, but not this time. It was painfully obvious the biggest attraction he held for Sherry was that he belonged to Olivia.

"Olivia still sleeping?"

Lucas looked up from his cup as Grace walked slowly into the kitchen and poured herself a cup of coffee from the pot on the stove. The hectic days were taking their toll on her too. "She's awake, but wanted to rest a while longer."

"How's she feeling this morning?"

"Better I think," he said, standing to pull out a chair for her. "At least she was last night. Mornings don't seem to be as good for her."

"Well, that's certainly understandable," Grace said, gingerly sipping at her cup.

"Understandable?" He gave his head a shake. "You mean for the flu?"

"No," she said, peeking at him from over the rim of her cup. "I mean understandable considering…everything."

Lucas knew the last few days had left him a little

punchy, but he had no idea what she was talking about. "Am I missing something here?"

"You two didn't think you could fool me, did you?"

Lucas sat up, dread turning his blood to ice. Grace knew—he could hear it in her voice and see it in her eyes. She knew everything—that there was no marriage, that it had all been an act, that he really wasn't married to her daughter.

"Oh, Grace...I—I don't know what to say. I feel so bad."

"Don't feel bad—and you don't have to say anything."

"But I'm...I'm so sorry."

"Lucas, dear," she said, setting down her cup and slipping a hand over his. "You have nothing to apologize for. I couldn't be happier."

He looked at her, the warm flush moving through his body. "What?"

"And you don't have to worry," she continued, giving his hand a squeeze. "I'll keep your secret."

"Y-you will?" he stammered, feeling like he'd gone to bed last night in the real world and woke up in the twilight zone.

"But I know that Monica would understand."

"Monica." Lucas ran a shaky hand along his forehead, trying to remember if he'd actually woke up this morning at all. Maybe this was all just a dream—a really, *really* bad one.

"I think it is so thoughtful that the two of you don't want take the attention away from her, but I know she wouldn't mind—she would be thrilled—everyone will be."

"Thrilled?" He took several deep breaths. "Grace, what are you talking about?"

"You don't have to pretend with me," she insisted, giving his hand a pat. "A mother knows her children and believe me, I knew the moment I looked at Olivia the other morning. I've been on the other side of that green face."

Grace was talking crazy. It almost sounded as if she thought—

A big, bright light bulb suddenly came on right above his head. "Oh, Grace, you don't think—"

She raised a hand, stopping him. "Now don't worry, I won't say anything—at least not until the two of you say it's okay."

"But, Grace—"

"No, no," she insisted, shaking her head. "You just take care of that wife of yours."

"But, Grace, you don't understand—"

"Oh, my dear boy, I understand far more than you realize." She set down her cup, her eyes sparkling with tears. She pushed out of her chair, walking around the table and wrapping her arms around his neck. "And just for your information, I couldn't be more thrilled." She kissed his cheek. "The whole family will be."

She turned and rushed out of the kitchen.

"But, Grace," he called after her, but she had already disappeared around the corner and down the hall.

Lucas stared at the empty doorway. Grace thought they were going to have a baby, she thought Olivia was pregnant. It was a crazy idea, absolutely crazy.

"Crazy," Lucas muttered as he started up the

stairs two at a time. Grace was just anxious for grandchildren—so anxious she was jumping to a lot of wrong conclusions. Or was she right? As he reached the top of the landing, he couldn't quite shake the feeling that it made a peculiar sort of sense. There was a lot he didn't know about Olivia Martin. Certainly if she was pregnant, it would explain her need for an instant husband and he still remembered her reaction that first day when Sherry asked her about starting a family.

He stopped, his mind racing. If there was a real baby that also meant there was a real father. Who was it and why wasn't he here with Olivia? Why wasn't he helping Grace in the kitchen and playing golf with Jacob? Why wasn't he with the woman who was carrying his child?

He made his way up the rest of the stairs and to the door of the bedroom feeling oddly betrayed. Maybe all the playacting and fantasy was finally getting to him. Maybe falling into the role of her husband had just become too easy, too comfortable and it was time for another reality check. The reality was that this woman wasn't his wife and if she was pregnant, it wasn't his child. Beyond that, all the rest was none of his business and one way or another he was going to have to remember that.

"You awake?" he asked, rapping lightly at the door as he opened it.

"I'm up," Olivia said dryly as she walked out of the bathroom in a cloud of steam, clad only in a robe and with her hair wrapped turban-style in a towel. "I'm just not sure I'm awake."

He watched as she moved past him and felt the

muscles in his stomach contract and knot tight. Was he just looking at her in a different light, or did she actually have a glow about her? She had been wearing that robe every morning for the last three days and there was certainly nothing alluring or revealing about it. But watching her now as she went sailing past him, she looked soft and warm and wholly feminine and he felt every fiber in his being stand up and take notice.

"Not feeling too good this morning?"

"Not too."

"You going to come down for breakfast?"

"I wasn't going to," she said, lifting a shoulder as she walked past him towards the bed. She reached up and pulled at the towel on her head, sending her hair falling down around her shoulders. "I thought I'd straighten up a bit around here and get a little rest. Besides, I'm not really hungry."

Watching her hair fall free, the knots in his stomach tightened even more. "You sure?"

She nodded. "Oh yeah, don't worry about me."

A clean, spicy fragrance floated about the room, invading his lungs and his blood "Because I, uh..." He swallowed hard, his mouth feeling dry and raw. "I could wait if you'd like to get dressed."

"That's okay," she assured him with a small laugh. She bent down and began straightening the comforter on the bed. "I'm not going to starve."

"Oh, uh, I know. I, uh, just thought that maybe..." He gave his head a shake. "Nothing, never mind."

She stopped as she fluffed the pillows. "Is everything okay?"

"Everything's fine," he insisted. "Just fine."

"You sure?"

"Absolutely." He sank his hands into the pockets of his jeans and walked to the window, leaning back against the windowsill. "I just thought I'd better tell you."

"Tell me what?"

"Something your mother said."

"Oh dear," Olivia groaned as she rounded the bed and walked towards him. "What did she say now?"

"Somehow she's gotten the idea that we're...I mean actually that you...that the two of us..."

"Lucas!"

"Okay, okay." He lifted his hands in surrender, realizing sometimes blurting things out was the only way. "Your mother doesn't think you have the flu."

"Oh?"

He shook his head. "She thinks you're going to have a baby."

Olivia felt her stomach lurch and roll over uneasily, but it had nothing to do with morning sickness this time. She listened as Lucas described the exchange he'd had with her mother and tried her best not to start ranting and raving in panic. Hysteria wasn't a luxury she could afford right now. She had to try and figure out what she was going to do. Nothing about this whole trip had gone as she'd planned—and now this. It was as if everything was unraveling before her very eyes.

Honesty is the best policy. The words of Mrs. Posner, her fourth grade teacher and Girl Scout leader, had been as true then as they were now and they were coming back to haunt her. Honesty—it was a concept she seemed to have forgotten about when she'd come up with this whole scheme. Despite the fact that her intentions were good, she'd been anything but honest and she'd been paying the price ever since.

As she listened to him, her mind raced, moving from one scenario to another, testing one excuse against another. She could always try and deny everything, laugh off her mother's suspicions and stick to her story of a bad bout with the flu, but it did seem silly to continue to deny what would soon be evident to everyone anyway. But the thought of adding yet another deception, another pretense to the mountain of untruths she'd told hardly seemed like the answer.

Then of course, she could just go downstairs and make the announcement. After all, she'd planned on telling her family soon anyway. What did it matter if it was now or in another week? *Yes, Mother, you're right, you guessed my little secret. You're going to be a grandma. I'm going to have a baby!* The only problem with this plan was that telling everyone now would also mean telling Lucas.

She really hadn't thought about how all this would play out once they both returned to Seattle. When she'd come up with the idea of hiring someone to portray her husband, she'd had a stranger in mind, some nameless, faceless person to fill the role and then disappear from her life once the job was done. But as the saying goes, that was then and this was now. Lucas McCall was hardly a random stranger. Besides being a mover and a shaker in the business world, he'd become someone real to her, someone with a name and a face and a smile she couldn't seem to stop thinking about. He was also someone whose opinion she was finding mattered a great deal to her.

In a few days the wedding would be over and they would be back in Seattle. The job would be done, their roles at an end and they would never have to see one another again. Was it really necessary that he have to know? Even though he had never actually said it, she knew he found it a little unusual she had told her parents she was married when she really wasn't. What would he do if he knew the whole story? What would he think of her then?

She closed her eyes, pinching at the tension building across the bridge of her nose. She'd asked him to be her husband, was it fair to ask him to be the father of her child too?

"I suppose it's a natural presumption," he concluded. "People get married and have kids—it's as simple as that. I just thought I'd better warn you."

"I appreciate it." She turned and walked to the closet, aware that he watched her as she moved. "I'll talk to my mother. Get things straightened out."

"So you're not then?"

She turned around. It would have been so easy to have just said no, so easy to have just made up another story like so many of the stories she'd been making up since they'd gotten there, but he looked at her with such an honest look of concern, with such caring, she couldn't bring herself to lie. He

deserved nothing short of the truth, and she owed it
to him.

"Actually...I am."

The look of shock in his eyes was almost more
than she could take and she quickly turned away.
She'd come to like the way he looked at her and
she wasn't up to seeing that change now. She didn't
want to think that she'd disappointed him, that he
would think any less of her. Reaching out a shaky
hand, she pulled open the closet door.

"I'm, uh, about twelve weeks. I was planning on
telling my family once I got back to Seattle." She
stopped and turned back to him. "I just thought it
would be less complicated—you know, for you."

"Well that explains it then," he said, pushing
himself away from the sill. "Why you needed a husband so fast."

"It seems ridiculous, I know," she said, pulling
clothes blindly from the closet. Her years as a physician may have made it possible to keep the emotion out of her voice, but it hadn't made it any easier. "I mean, at my age to be concerned about
shocking your parents, but you can see how my
folks are—stodgy, conservative. They just wouldn't
have understood."

"I think you might be selling them short."

She shrugged, giving her head a shake. "Maybe,
I don't know. I just didn't want it to affect how
they'd feel about the child."

"It's their grandchild. I know them well enough
to know they're going to love a child of yours no
matter what."

He was right of course, except this child wasn't

her child—this was Rachel and Ted's child. They may feel differently about that.

"I know," she said with a sigh, putting some of the clothes she'd removed back on the shelf. "I was just trying to do what I thought was best for everyone."

"So you made up a husband."

She nodded. "Right."

"What about the baby's father? You couldn't ask him?"

It was right there—the truth. All she had to do was open her mouth and say it. She could just tell him about the arrangement she had made with Rachel and Ted and how she'd become the surrogate mother to a child who had become her own. She could toss it all out on the table and let the pieces fall where they may.

Only...when she opened her mouth to speak, the words simply were not there.

"Things..." she started, her voice deserting her. Clearing her throat loudly, she tried again. "Things didn't work as we'd planned," she said, telling herself she wasn't exactly being untruthful with him. "He's no longer in the picture."

"I see."

He didn't see. He didn't see any of it, but it was all she could tell him without reverting to more pretense and half-truths—something she couldn't seem to bring herself to do.

"You could have told me you know."

She looked up at him, telling herself what she saw in his eyes wasn't disappointment, wasn't disillusionment. "I was just trying to work on the marriage thing. I was hoping I wouldn't have to start in on the family thing for awhile."

"So does that mean you're going to tell your mother she's right?"

No, it was disappointment and it was disillusionment and it was as plain as day. Why hadn't she just called that escort service back? Why hadn't she just hired some blond hunk with a pretty face, someone she didn't care about, someone who wouldn't have looked at her and made her *feel* something? "I haven't figured that out yet."

"You mean I can't tell anyone?" Grace complained, reaching out and pushing Olivia's hair back from her forehead. "Not even your father?"

"You can tell Daddy, but let's wait at least until after the wedding," Olivia pleaded. She looked up into her mother's tear-stained face and felt like crying herself. Her mother sat propped against the pillows along the headboard while she stretched out across the bed. The two of them had been talking alone in Grace's bedroom for the better part of an hour—talking in the way they had done a hundred times when she'd been growing up and Olivia knew this would be one of those talks she would always remember.

Grace had bubbled at the thought of becoming a grandmother and Olivia found her mother's excitement and enthusiasm contagious. She'd accepted the fact intellectually that she was going to have a baby, but she didn't think she'd actually realized it emotionally until now—*she was going to have a baby!*

"This is Monica's time," she continued, the lump

in her throat making the words difficult. "Let's not spoil it for her."

"Spoil it?" Grace scoffed. "How could news like this spoil anything?"

She gave her mother a knowing look. "You know what I mean. Besides, I think I want to keep this to myself awhile longer."

"Okay," Grace reluctantly conceded. "But I have to tell you, there's a bit of talk going on."

Olivia frowned. "What do you mean?"

"I'm not the only one who has put two and two together," Grace insisted. "Both Kate and Kathleen suspect something is up—and of course Sherry. You know nothing escapes her."

Olivia groaned. "Oh great."

"I think the whole family is a little anxious for the pitter-patter of little feet."

"Well, could we just keep this between us for awhile longer anyway?"

"If that's what you want," Grace groused with a heavy sigh. "What does Lucas say?"

Olivia felt a chill despite the warm California weather. "Lucas wants what I want."

There must have been something in her voice, something in her expression because no sooner were the words out of her mouth than Grace's smile faded. She turned a shrewd gaze to her daughter, perusing her carefully.

"Olivia, what is it?"

She might be able to get away with fudging the truth to her mother long distance, but face-to-face she was a goner. Every word sounded guilty and wholly unbelievable even to herself.

"You're not telling me something," Grace insisted. "I know. I can tell." She sat upright on the bed. "Is everything all right? I mean, is the baby okay?"

Olivia really hadn't intended on saying anything—not right then anyway, not after the nice talk they'd been having but now that the opportunity had just sort of presented itself, it would be foolish to let it slip by. Sooner rather than later she would have to break the news to everyone that her marriage to Lucas had ended. She didn't have to blurt out everything, but sowing a few seeds now wouldn't hurt and just might make the announcement a little easier later on.

"The baby's fine, Mom," Olivia quickly assured her.

"But there is something, isn't there? Something else."

"Yes." She nodded, nervously twisting the corner of the bedspread. "I—I don't really want to talk about it—I can't. It's just that Lucas and I...well..."

"You and Lucas what?" Grace prompted.

Olivia turned away. This was not something she could do face-to-face. "Things happened pretty fast with us, you know that. Meeting the way we did, getting married and now the baby—we've hardly had time to get used to one another. We've just got some things we need to work out."

She felt her mother's hand on her shoulder and it was all she could do to stop herself from bursting into tears. She was sick of the falsehoods and the half-truths, sick of evading issues and creating misconceptions. At that moment she swore an oath that once this whole nightmare was over, she would never tell another lie again.

"I won't pry," Grace finally said in a low voice after a long silence. "I know the early months in a marriage can be difficult with so many changes and you both have to make adjustments." She gathered the long locks of Olivia's hair in her hands, smoothing it back away from her face, a comfortable, familiar gesture that mothers and daughters the world around come to know and take solace in. "But you'll work things out—I know it. And just remember Lucas loves you—a blind man can see that."

Chapter Eight

"Are you sure you're feeling up to going tonight, Olivia dear? You still look a little green around the gills to me."

Olivia finished drying the stoneware plate and slipped it on to the top of the stack inside the cupboard. Between her bouts of morning sickness and all the other wedding activities, she'd managed to avoid Sherry for most of the week, but her luck had run out now. Sherry had floated in about an hour ago, and had been her shadow ever since.

"I'm feeling just fine," she said dryly, Sherry's concern not fooling her for a moment. "I'm sure I'll be able to struggle through the evening somehow."

"Okay," Sherry said, sounding skeptical. "But I'd just hate to see you get to the restaurant and have another relapse."

Olivia tossed the damp towel over the wooden dish rack on the counter and untied the apron around her waist. "Well, I appreciate the concern, Sherry, I really do, but it's just a rehearsal dinner—not a command performance in front of the royal family. If I start to feel bad, I'll just come home."

"Whatever you say," Sherry said with a casual shrug. "I'm just so sorry I couldn't have been more help with those dishes, but that water is just a killer on my nails. Doesn't it bother yours?"

She held out her hands, displaying ten perfectly-shaped, perfectly-painted, inch-plus nails that just happened, by a bizarre coincidence, to look like a lethal set of claws.

"No, Sherry, I'm afraid my patients would mutiny if I was to come at them with a set of nails like that."

"I forgot you deliver babies all day long." Sherry hesitated for about a millisecond before adding "So, now that we're alone, tell me when you're going to have one of your own."

As a doctor, Olivia would have said it was medically impossible to feel flushed and have chills at the same time, but at that moment she was living proof that it could be done.

"I don't know. It'll happen when it happens."

"Well, I can't believe you and Lucas haven't discussed it," Sherry continued. "I mean, you're married. It's only natural to think of starting a family."

"Oh, really?" Despite her peculiar bout of hot chills, Olivia decided maybe it was time for Sherry to see how she liked it on the hot seat. "Did you think of that during your two marriages?"

The look of annoyance that flashed through

Sherry's eyes was subtle, but Olivia recognized it for what it was—set point.

"I would have loved to have had children with either one of my husbands," Sherry said coolly. "Unfortunately I wasn't able to conceive when I was with John—and if I'd known I was going to lose poor Clarence as soon as I did, maybe we wouldn't have waited before trying to start a family."

"Sherry, you couldn't conceive with John because you insisted he have a vasectomy before you'd agree to marry him and Clarence was eighty-seven when the two of you got married. How long had you planned on waiting?"

"Well now you're just being mean," Sherry pouted, looking more self-satisfied than insulted. "And it's all because of Charles isn't it. You're still angry about that, aren't you—that's why you're striking out."

Why was she striking out? Maybe Sherry's competitiveness had bothered her once, but no more. Now her bragging and one-upping just seemed a sad and pathetic ploy to gain attention and mask a very insecure person.

"Oh, Sherry, I'm sorry," she said, feeling emancipated and freer than she ever could remember. "I was just trying to point out that when to start a family is something every couple comes to in their own time and in their own way. Charles and all of that is history—*ancient* history."

There must have been something in her manner or in her tone that made it clear she meant what she said because something in Sherry's smug expression faded and died for good.

"Uh, well, good. I'm...I'm glad to hear that," Sherry stammered, relinquishing the point of leverage with some reluctance. "And I would have thought you'd be anxious for a child—you do plan on having children, don't you?"

"I would love to have a family someday," Olivia said with conviction.

"Someday," Sherry repeated, giving her a skeptical look. "No sooner than that?"

"I'm not exactly following a timetable," Olivia pointed out.

"Would Lucas rather wait?"

"Tell you what, Sherry. Why don't you ask him next time you see him?"

"I think I will," Sherry beamed, looking smug once again. "I'll do that. Where is he, by the way? I haven't seen him all morning."

Olivia felt her blood pressure inch up a degree and reminded herself Lucas McCall wasn't really her husband and if she felt any jealousy at all it was not only because of hormones, it was because she was a fool too. "He's taken Maury and the boys over to the tailor to pick up their tuxes. They're liable to be gone for a while."

"Hey, Mom! Mom! Where are you?" Kevin burst into the kitchen as if on cue, racing around the counter. "Hey, Olivia, where's my mom?"

"She's upstairs," Olivia stammered, barely having time to point in the general direction of the stairs before he started off again. "Hey, when did you guys get back?"

"Just now," he said as he raced back out the door and disappeared around the corner.

Olivia's gaze shifted to Sherry, who stood there smiling as though she held a winning lotto ticket. "Well, I guess you'll be able to ask Lucas anything you want."

"Ask me what?"

Lucas stood in the doorway, and suddenly Olivia felt as though all of the oxygen had been sucked out of the room.

"Lucas!" Sherry screeched like a teenybopper spotting her favorite teen idol. "It's about time."

Olivia felt something very hot and very unpleasant shoot through her system as she watched Sherry sail across the kitchen and slip her arm through Lucas's. She may have laid her past with Sherry to rest—all those memories of competition and rivalry and Charles—but where Lucas McCall was concerned, she definitely had a ways to go.

Lucas looked down at Sherry clinging to his lifeless arm, then lifted his gaze to Olivia. "Did you need me for something?"

"She didn't, but I did," Sherry answered quickly, tugging at his arm until he looked at her again. "I wanted to ask you something."

Lucas glanced at Olivia again. "Oh really? And what might that be?"

"Well your wife doesn't seem to want to talk about it, so I'll ask you," Sherry said, tugging at his arm again. "Tell me Lucas, are you anxious to become a daddy?"

The look of surprise on Lucas's face was clear

and Olivia felt her blood begin to simmer once again. Leave it to Sherry to stir things up.

"When...the time is right," he said after a moment, shooting Olivia a look that sent her temperature rising for an entirely different reason. "I'll be more than ready."

"I've got something to tell you."

Olivia eased the brush through Monica's hair and glanced at her reflection in the mirror. "So tell me."

"First you have to promise you won't get upset."

"Upset? Upset about what?"

"Promise first."

Olivia reached for a skinny hot roller and curled one of Monica's short honey-colored locks around it. "Why do I get the feeling you're about to tell me you ruined my favorite sweater you borrowed without asking."

"I asked," Monica mocked, playacting the argument they'd had dozens of times as teens. "Well, I *meant* to."

"Uh-huh," Olivia nodded, her smile growing wide. "Now the truth comes out."

Monica smiled, but when she turned in her chair and reached for Olivia's hand, her smile faded. "But now I want you to promise."

Olivia's smile faded too. The look on her sister's face made her know this wasn't a joking matter. "Monica, what is it?"

"Olivia," she said, tears springing to her eyes. "I know about the baby—"

"Oh, no," Olivia groaned.

"No, please, Olivia. Don't be upset," Monica pleaded, shaking her head.

"Mom promised she wouldn't say anything."

"And she didn't," Monica insisted. "She didn't have to."

"Oh, Monica," Olivia sighed, tears springing alive in her eyes too and spilling down her cheeks. "Can you believe it? I'm going to have a baby."

"I know," Monica sobbed, pulling Olivia into her arms. "Isn't that something?"

Olivia wasn't sure how long they stood there hugging and crying, but it was long enough to leave them both exhausted. When she finally stepped back, her eyes felt as red and swollen as Monica's looked.

"And don't be upset with Mom—I confronted her and made her tell me," Monica insisted. "She did say though that there was some strain…you know, between you and Lucas."

"Things are going to be fine," Olivia answered stoically. "Don't worry about us." In an effort to change the subject, she pointed to their images in the mirror. "Oh my goodness will you look at us. If we don't finish with these hot rollers, you really are going to have a bad hair day."

"I don't care," Monica said, grabbing a handful of tissues from the box on the vanity and dividing them between herself and her sister. "I'm too happy to be concerned about what I look like."

"Well you won't feel that way when the photographer points that camera at you."

Monica gave herself a look in the mirror and cringed. "No, I suppose you're right."

"I would have told you about the baby," Olivia began as she reached for the hairbrush again. "After the wedding. I just didn't want to spoil anything...you know, this special time..."

"Oh, Olivia," Monica said, tears threatening her eyes again. "I appreciate that, I really do, but you should have known Peter and I would have been thrilled for you and...and Lucas." Her smile suddenly faltered and she grasped at Olivia's hand. "Things are going to be all right with you two, aren't they?"

Olivia squeezed her sister's hand, hating the lies and hating herself for having told them. "I hope so."

"Because you two seem so perfect together, so happy."

Olivia struggled to dislodge the lump in her throat. "Let's not talk about this now. There will be time for all that later, okay?" Monica nodded, but there was something in her expression that had Olivia stopping as she reached for another roller. "What is it?" She turned and faced her sister. "There's something else, isn't there?"

Monica looked sick as she nodded. "It's Sherry. She sort of...knows too?"

The hairbrush dropped from Olivia's hand. *"What?"*

"You promised you wouldn't get upset."

"No, I didn't. I didn't promise anything." Olivia experienced another peculiar episode of hot chills. "How did that happen?"

"You know how Sherry is, always managing to show up when you aren't expecting her," Monica complained. "She was outside in the hall when Mom and I were talking. And with Sherry having no scruples, she listened." She reached out and put a hand on Olivia's shoulder. "I hope you're not too upset."

Olivia drew in a deep breath. This was not turning out to be one of her favorite days. It was barely half over and yet already she had ran the gamut of emotions. To say things weren't working out as she'd planned was an understatement, but that didn't mean they weren't working out. The order might have been skewed by circumstance and unplanned events, but she'd still managed to do what she'd set out to do—introduced her family to her husband, let them know a child was on the way and drop hints of trouble in the marriage. Now it was time to stop worrying about herself and concentrate on making this time special for Monica.

"I'm not," she said, feeling almost relieved. "And I guess everyone's got to know sooner or later—why not let Sherry tell them?"

Monica pushed away a tear, looking so relieved she actually laughed. "Hey, she's told the family everything else that's ever happened to us—why not this, right?"

It was so ridiculous, and so true, Olivia laughed too. "Right. Now let's get this hair of yours set before she starts telling everyone about that too, okay?"

"Oh, Olivia," Monica sighed, pulling her sister into her arms. "I'm so happy and I want you to be happy too."

"I'm working on it, little sister," Olivia assured her, blinking away the tears. "I'm working on it."

"I wish you'd warned me."

Olivia lifted the iron from her dress, but refused to look in his direction. The image of him standing there in front of the mirror with his chest bare, wearing only blue jeans and looking like one of those male models from a shaving commercial was already permanently seared into her brain.

"When would you have suggested I do that?" she asked, setting the iron down and repositioning the dress on the ironing board.

Lucas peered through the open bathroom doorway, his razor poised in his hand. "Sometime before people began congratulating me."

Olivia picked up the iron again and carefully slid it along the luxurious black silk. The afternoon had been no less hectic than the morning, and no less emotional. Sherry had taken the news of the baby and ran with it and soon everyone in the family knew. Congratulations and good wishes had come in all afternoon along with the requisite hugs and kisses. Unfortunately, there had been no time to fill Lucas in on everything so he'd come home from having run errands with Peter and been hit with a round of hearty congratulations.

"That might have been a little difficult with Sherry draped on your arm in the kitchen, or when the two of you went off to the driving range together."

Lucas made a face through the shaving cream.

"We hardly went together. I went with your father, she just happened to tag along."

Olivia shrugged a little too casually but it helped cover the swell of anger that rose in her throat. She just had to concentrate on getting through the rehearsal dinner tonight and the wedding tomorrow and then she'd be able to put all this insane jealousy and possessiveness to rest once and for all.

"Whatever. My point was only that we haven't exactly had a chance to talk alone."

Lucas shifted his gaze to his image in the mirror, leaning over the sink and swiping the razor down his cheek. "Well, we're alone now. Are there any other bombshells I should know about?"

Olivia lowered the iron again. "Well, now that you mention it."

Lucas reached for the knob on the faucet and turned it off. "What is it?"

Breaking her vow, she turned and looked at him. "I also planted a few seeds."

"Seeds?"

"Hints, you know," she said, quickly looking away. "About the divorce."

"Oh?"

Something in the tone of his voice had her looking up again. Even behind a mask of shaving cream, she could see his expression go rigid. "The opportunity just sort of came up."

"With who?"

"My mother," she said, telling herself she had absolutely no reason to feel guilty. She slipped her dress from the ironing board and on to a satin covered hanger.

"So you told your mother we were going to have a baby and then you told her we're getting a divorce?"

"No," she insisted, wondering why she felt so defensive. After all, a divorce had been in the plan all along. "I told you, I just planted a few seeds, just hinted that we were having a few second thoughts, that's all." She adjusted the dress on the hanger and pulled the zipper into place. "I'm sure everyone knows all about that too, thanks to Sherry."

"Well that might explain a few things then," he said after a moment, reaching down and turning the faucet back on.

"What things?"

He looked back at his reflection in the mirror. "Something your father said."

"My father?" She hung the dress on a hook beside the matching jacket. "What did he say?"

"Something about not taking things too seriously right now." He moved the razor down his other cheek. "That women in your condition can be a little difficult."

"Difficult?" Olivia stopped as she reached for her shoes on the top shelf of the closet. "My father said that?"

Lucas contorted his lower lip, maneuvering the razor along his chin. "Actually I think the word he used was testy."

"Testy," she muttered, grabbing the black heels and slipping them on her stockinged feet. She stalked across the room towards the bathroom, the black hose and heels looking all the more out of place beneath her ratty terry robe. She squeezed carefully past Lucas, telling herself skin was just skin and the fact that his had brushed hers meant nothing at all. "And if we are—" She stopped and shot him a look in the mirror. "—*testy*, it's only because the men in our lives make stupid comments like that."

Lucas's dark gaze found hers in the mirror. "A little touchy aren't we?" He paused for a second as he moved to rinse the razor again. "And notice I didn't say testy."

"Well if I'm a little touchy, it's not without reason," she insisted, feeling defensive again. "I'm a little tired of being the subject of conversation around here."

He pulled the towel from around his neck and wiped away what tiny flecks of shaving cream remained. "You can't blame your family for caring. A baby is big news—so is a troubled marriage, for that matter. They're just concerned about you."

"Don't defend them," she snapped, unzipping her makeup bag and pulling out a long tube of mascara. "What about respecting a person's privacy? What about people just plain minding their own business?"

"They're your family, maybe they think it is their business."

She swiped furiously at her lashes. "Oh my, yes. Sherry doesn't seem to have any qualms about sticking her nose into other people's business."

"Well, I don't know that I'd put your cousin Sherry in the same category as the rest of your family."

"Oh, no?" She tossed the tube back into her makeup bag and reached for her hairbrush. "Just what category would you put her in?"

Lucas tossed the towel over the shower door and walked out of the bathroom. "Some place different than Monica and your parents."

She watched as he walked out of the bathroom. She pulled the brush through her hair with such vengeance it nearly brought tears to her eyes. "Well, I know where she'd like to put you."

He hung his shirt on a hook next to her dress. "Really?"

"Oh, come on, Lucas," she said, slamming the hairbrush back into the bag and stalking back out of the bathroom. "You know what she's doing."

He reached back into the closet, pulling out a hanger with a pair of charcoal wool slacks draped over it. "I do?"

"Lucas," she scoffed, unzipping a pocket of her suitcase and fishing out a small, flat velvet box. "She's been gushing all over you since the moment we got here."

Lucas reached into a garment bag and pulled out a gray tweed blazer. "So?"

"So don't tell me you don't know."

He stopped and gave his head a shake. "What are you talking about?"

Olivia opened the velvet box and took out the strand of pearls from inside. "We're talking about you and Sherry."

He shook his head. "No, that's what *you're* talking about. *I* was talking about your family caring about you."

Olivia felt her face flush florid. They might not be married, but she sure had a way of sounding like a jealous wife. "Look, can we just drop this? If we don't finish getting ready we're going to be late for the rehearsal dinner."

"Sure, whatever you say," he said, grabbing a black turtleneck sweater from inside his suitcase and sliding it on over his head. "And I'm sorry if I said something to upset you."

"It's not you," she said with a sigh, slipping the pearls around her neck. "I'm sorry if I am a little...touchy."

"There you go, apologizing again," he said, pulling the turtleneck into place and spotting her struggling to close the necklace. "And let me help you with that."

"Thanks," she said, lifting her hair to give him access to the clasp. "And I am sorry. Like I said before, this whole week has been difficult."

"And like your father said, women in your condition..."

She turned and gave him a deliberate look. "Careful. I don't think we want to go there again."

"I only meant," he added quickly. "You know, like he said, women can be emotional when they're going to have babies."

"I thought he said testy."

Lucas leaned close. "I was being diplomatic."

She breathed out a small laugh. "I think you're learning."

"He said your mother was very *emotional* during her pregnancies." Lucas slipped the small gold hook through the clasp, securing the pearls in place. "And you're just like your mother."

Olivia wasn't sure why, but the words hit her in the face like a bucket of ice water. She loved and respected her mother, but anyone could see they were nothing alike—nothing!

"What?" She whirled around, her hair flying, and glared up at him. "What's that supposed to mean?"

"I, uh—" he stammered, his eyes wide with surprise. "N-nothing—"

She pushed his hands away, stalking towards the closet and yanking her dress from the hanger. "That must have been some talk you two had."

"Olivia, look, I don't know—"

"And tell me," she demanded, tossing off her robe and stepping into the silk dress. "Just how much did Sherry contribute to this little conversation?"

He reached for his slacks, sliding them off the hanger. "Sherry? Why are we talking about her again."

"Because she sure seems to have an awful lot to say to you where I'm concerned."

Lucas tossed his jeans on to the bed and stepped into his slacks. "I don't know what you're talking about."

"Oh, please, you know exactly what I'm talking about." She twisted and struggled, reaching for the zipper at the back of her dress.

"You keep saying that," he said, taking her by the shoulders and turning her around none too gently. He caught the tab of her zipper, yanking it up in one fluid motion.

The dress felt snug and uncomfortable around the waist, which only made her that much angrier. "I keep saying it because it's true."

He stepped into black leather loafers. "That's just crazy."

"Oh, so now I'm crazy," she huffed, struggling to suck in her tummy. She walked to the closet and snatched the matching jacket from the hanger. "Let's see, first testy, then touchy, now crazy."

"No," he said, stalking towards the door. Twisting the knob, he yanked the door open, stepping to one side in order to let her pass. "Just crazy. Just plain crazy."

Olivia came to an abrupt halt in the middle of the room. She stood there staring at him as he held the door for her, the full import of what had just happened hitting her square in the face.

"Oh, my God," she gasped, grabbing at her jacket and clutching it across herself as though it were a towel and she'd just stepped from the shower. "Oh, my God!"

"What?"

"Look at us" she demanded, pointing at him and then herself. "Will you look at us."

His gaze bounced between them before turning helplessly to her again. "What? What's the matter?"

"We—we're *dressed*," she shrieked.

Lucas looked down at his turtleneck and slacks, realizing what it was she was trying to tell him. "We're dressed."

Olivia stared at him, hardly able to believe what she was seeing. Could she have been that distracted?

Could she honestly have been so caught up in the arguing she hadn't even noticed? Somehow, some way, through the angry outbursts and emotional explosions they both had managed to change into their good clothes—right in front of one another.

Chapter Nine

"You know, sweetheart, your Uncle Maury and I fought like cats and dogs those first months," Kathleen said in a low voice. "I swear, if we hadn't been so broke, I think I would have left him." She leaned back in her chair, watching her husband as he sat nodding in a chair in the corner despite the noise and commotion of the restaurant. "But he needed help at the dry cleaners and I didn't have a job so I guess we were stuck with each other." Turning back, she lifted a hand to Olivia's cheek. "Those early times were rough, but I think that's what kept us together all these years."

Olivia smiled at her aunt. She appreciated the thinly veiled advice, but she wasn't sure how much more she could take. The wedding rehearsal had gone smoothly enough, but the dinner was proving endless. It was painfully evident that the seed she had planted had grown and blossomed far more than she'd expected. As word of her troubled marriage had spread among the family, she'd been forced to endure one not-so-subtle dose of advice after another from one well-meaning relative after another. While she appreciated the concern, she wished now she had never said anything at all. After five long days, she felt bad enough playing out this whole farce without being forced into the position of trying to save a marriage that didn't exist.

"Aunt Kathleen, you haven't met Peter's brother from Sacramento yet, have you?" Monica asked, rushing to the table.

"I don't believe so, dear."

"Oh come, please," she coaxed, taking her aunt's hand. "I'll introduce you."

"Oh, of course, I'd love to," Kathleen said, reaching for her handbag from under her chair. "Let me just go freshen up a bit."

"Okay, I'll wait right here," Monica called after her as she rushed to the powder room. Leaning down, she gave Olivia a sympathetic pat on the shoulders. "You looked as though you could use a break."

"Was it that obvious?"

"Only to your baby sister. How you doing?"

"I'm doing fine except my dress is cutting off my circulation to the lower half of my body," Olivia said, looking up at her sister and giving her a phony smile. "But you don't have to worry about me. I'm fine."

Monica gave her a skeptical look. "Actually, you look a little tired."

"I'm fine—trust me, I'm a doctor, I know these

things.'' She reached up and patted Monica's hand on her shoulder. ''Now there's Aunt Kathleen, go get her—*please*.''

''Okay, but you know, if you wanted to cut out of here a little early, I'm sure everyone would understand.''

''You not feeling good?''

Olivia jumped at the sound of Lucas's voice behind her. She'd done a fairly good job of avoiding him this evening, not that she thought he'd even noticed. Sherry had no doubt gotten wind of their marriage woes as she hadn't left his side since they'd gotten there. But the way she felt right now, that was just fine with her. She wished she could just go on avoiding him indefinitely. It mortified her to think about what had happened in the bedroom. The argument had been bad enough with her acting like some kind of jealous maniac, but to think that she'd actually undressed in front of him was just too much. And besides that, next to Sherry's tiny, little strapless dress, her silk suit looked old, outdated and too tight to boot.

''I'm fine,'' she said over her shoulder, careful not to look directly at him.

''Lucas, I think your wife looks exhausted,'' Monica said, spotting Aunt Kathleen coming towards them and moving to head her off. ''Maybe you can talk her into going home early.''

They both watched as Monica took off between the tables and steered Kathleen in the opposite direction.

''I could, you know,'' Lucas said, pulling out the

chair vacated by Kathleen and sitting down. "Take you home, I mean. Just say the word."

"I appreciate it," she said, pulling her jacket closed in hopes that he wouldn't notice her protruding tummy. "But I think I'd like to stay a little longer."

"Could I get you something to drink? A soft drink maybe? A cup of tea?"

How could he do that? How could he sit there and be so nice to her when she had behaved so badly? She'd said some terrible things to him, had acted like a jealous shrew and had all but accused him of wanting to leave her for Sherry. How had he kept from laughing? She was beyond embarrassed, she was mortified. Why couldn't he just go away and forget she even existed?

"No, thanks, I'm fine."

"Something to eat then? Remember, you're eating for two now."

He'd been nothing but thoughtful and good-natured through this whole ordeal and she couldn't remember having behaved this badly in her life. Not only had she been testy, touchy and jealous, she'd been dishonest as well. She didn't even want to think about what he must make of all this. First she'd told her parents she was married when she wasn't, then she'd told them he was the father of her child, which he wasn't. It all must sound crazy to him, because it sounded that way to her. Still, he hadn't pushed her for answers, hadn't probed or prodded. He'd respected her privacy, even when it meant having to play the role of the proud papa. What would he do if she were to tell him the truth, if she were to explain the rhyme and the reason for her madness? Would he understand, or would he think she was a bigger nutcase than he thought already?

"No, no," she said, shaking her head. "No thanks."

She experienced only a brief moment of panic then, thinking she might actually be expected to carry on a conversation with him. How was she suppose to sit there and chitchat with the man when she was too humiliated to look him in the eyes? But her panic was short-lived. Lucas had no more sat down than her father came rushing to their table.

"Okay, you two, you're next."

"Next for what?" Olivia demanded, still feeling a little annoyed by his testy comment.

"Pictures," he said, motioning for them to stand. "The photographer is waiting." Taking advantage of having their family together, he and Grace had requested that formal photos of everyone be taken. Taking several steps backwards, he motioned again for them to follow. "Come on, he's waiting."

Lucas looked at Olivia and shrugged. Standing, he gallantly put a hand on her chair. "Shall we?"

Olivia felt every eye on her as they walked through the crowded room to where the photographer had set up his equipment. It was bad enough to think everyone had been discussing them, but to feel dowdy and unattractive in a dress that was too tight only made it that much worse.

The photographer had the kind of polished, professional charm that came from having spent years working with people. He joked and clowned around

with them, succeeding in making everyone laugh—
except Olivia and Lucas. He positioned them in several different poses, coaxing them to smile and hold
hands and say cheese as he snapped picture after
picture. Olivia cooperated as best she could, but with
Lucas sitting so close, with their knees touching and
his hand holding hers, it was a struggle.

"Okay," the photographer finally said, adjusting
the lens on the camera as he peered through the
viewfinder. "Just one more for the scrapbook." He
looked up, giving Lucas a smile. "How about giving
that lovely wife of yours a nice kiss."

"What?" Olivia gasped. Just when she thought
things couldn't get any worse, just when she thought
she'd been as embarrassed or as uncomfortable as
she ever could be, it always seemed to get worse.
"I—I don't think so."

"Oh, come on, Olivia," her cousin Robyn called
out, giving her husband Sam, a hug. "He's made us
all do it."

"Come on," Maury shouted out. "Don't tell me
you're shy."

Olivia felt Lucas's strong hand on hers and she
looked up at him. They'd had plenty of awkward
moments in the last six days, but nothing like this.
She wanted to say something, wanted to make some
suggestion, offer some excuse that would help get
them out of this. But something happened when she
looked up into his eyes, something that had her forgetting about what she'd been going to say, that had
her forgetting about the others, laughing and joking
around them, and about the camera lens pointed
their way.

He looked at her with dark, hungry eyes that seemed to reach within her and bring to life needs and emotions she had tried so desperately to ignore. At that moment, it didn't matter what parts they were playing or what roles had been assigned, what illusion had been created and what pretense had been enacted. The only thing that mattered was what she saw in his eyes, and that what she saw was real.

"Lucas," she murmured as he lowered his mouth to hers.

It was as if everything had come to a stop, as if the world suddenly ceased spinning and life came to an abrupt halt. For that moment there was no wind, no water, no earth, no sky—no other reality outside of Lucas and Olivia, outside of his lips on hers. She found herself lost in the kiss, lost in a way she had never known, lost in a way that made her never want to find her way back.

His arm slipped around her waist, pulling her close, but for her it wasn't close enough. His taste tore through her like a powerful and potent drug, ripping at her veins and turning her blood to fire. The more he demanded, the more she provided, the more she couldn't seem to get enough. This wasn't a kiss, it was a challenge, a summons, daring and enticing her, making her cry out for more.

By the time he pulled his mouth away, they both were breathing hard. Olivia wasn't sure how much time had elapsed—a moment, an hour, an eon—but instinctively she knew that if there had been any gossip of problems in their marriage, they'd managed to put them to rest.

"Man," murmured the photographer, pulling out

a handkerchief from inside his jacket and wiping at his brow. "That was one heck of a shot."

Lucas rubbed at the tension building between his eyes. It was almost over. In less than twelve hours they would be on a plane heading back for Seattle and his life would be his own again. The wedding was beautiful and watching as Monica and Peter danced together, it was evident they were blissfully happy. But he felt a little like he'd been fighting his way through a war zone—and he was still deep in enemy territory.

It may have been Monica's day, and she had made a beautiful bride, but as far as he'd been concerned, there had been no other woman in that church but Olivia. She had looked breathtaking and everything in him had responded to that. Watching her he realized he had spent too long playacting, spent too long pretending to be the man in her life. Either that, or he simply had begun to enjoy torturing himself because as she made her way along the procession, he couldn't help imagining what it might be like if she were his bride, carrying his child and she was walking down the aisle to him. It was stupid to think like that, stupid to get so caught up in a pretense that could only cause him emotional agony, but there didn't seem to be much he could do to stop it. He'd gone completely overboard for the woman.

It was that kiss—the kiss to end all kisses. It had made him crazy, nuts, totally wacko. He couldn't seem to stop thinking about it, couldn't seem to stop thinking about her—the taste of her lips, the scent of her perfume, the feel of her hand, the softness of her skin, the silkiness of her hair—he could go on and on. He'd become completely caught up in the woman and it had to stop—*he* had to stop, had to get away from all this and get some perspective on things. He was drowning in the woman, in the family, in a marriage that didn't even exist. It wasn't that he wanted it to be over, that he wanted to get back to his life in Seattle, he *had* to before he made a complete fool of himself.

The night had been torture, but then each of the last six nights had been—each worse than the other. Still, he had no one but himself to blame. He'd ridden to the rescue, had become the knight rescuing the fair damsel in distress, but now he needed someone to rescue him, someone to pull him out because he was completely over his head.

He'd almost made it—almost. Last night at the wedding rehearsal, he'd begun to see light at the end of the tunnel. He'd made it through the grueling week, but it was almost over and he'd practically been home free. But that's where he'd made his mistake. He'd begun to relax, begun to drop his guard. That was the only explanation he had, the only reason he could think of to explain what he'd done. If he'd been thinking, if his brain had been functioning instead of turning to mush whenever he got near her he never would have kissed her like that, never would have allowed himself to get so far afield of the truth, or be so tempted to stray into the fantasy. But she had looked so exhausted last night, so fragile it had made him feel like such a heel for having argued with her.

He thought of how shocked she had been when she'd realized they changed their clothes in front of one another and had to admit he'd been pretty shocked himself. Maybe it was bound to happen— or something like it. As far as he was concerned, the longer they pretended to be married, the more difficulty he was having finding where the pretense ended and reality began. But it had been painfully obvious to him that she didn't exactly feel the same way. She'd barely spoken to him since then, and ever since the kiss, she hadn't even been able to bring herself to look at him.

"May I have this dance?"

He looked up, surprised to see her standing in front of him. He didn't know if he believed in the existence of angels, but looking at her now he knew if the creatures existed at all they had nothing on her. She looked serene, ravishing and utterly radiant.

"Me?" Lucas jumped awkwardly to his feet. "Sure. I—I'd love to."

He placed a hesitant hand at the small of her back as they made their way through the crowded tent to the dance floor. The music was slow and rhythmic, and the huge glass ball suspended from one of the tent's beams over the center of the dance floor sent tiny specks of light traveling wildly about in all directions. As they moved with the music, they glided with the rest of the crowd becoming one sea of motion, light, sound and music.

"I just wanted to say thank you," she said, pulling back just far enough to look up at him. "I know this last week hasn't been easy."

He shrugged a shoulder. "You never promised easy."

She smiled. "Maybe not, but..." Her smile slowly faded. "But it turned out to be more difficult than I'd expected and I'm really sorry."

"You're apologizing again."

"I guess I am," she said, smiling again. "But I did want to tell you how much I appreciated everything you did. I know it wasn't easy to deal with." She paused, glancing away. "I know I wasn't easy to deal with."

The gentle sway of their bodies together made it difficult for him to concentrate. He wanted to tell her how wonderful she was, wanted her to know how much this week had meant to him, how nice he thought her family was and how he wished he really could be a part of it. But that was crazy thinking. It would only embarrass her and make him sound like a fool. He'd become too caught up in the role he was playing, imagining what it would be like if they really were married. If he wasn't careful he'd start thinking he was in love with her or something. He had to hang on for just a little while longer. One more night and he'd be back in Seattle.

"You were a tyrant, I know," he joked, playfully making a face and shivering. "Terrible."

She laughed. "Well thank you for agreeing so quickly."

He wanted to laugh, he wanted to joke and tease and clown around, but when he looked at her he felt anything but playful. He had to steer clear of her, had to find something—a subject or a topic of some kind that he could discuss with her that wouldn't have his mind fantasizing and his body following suit.

"It was a beautiful wedding," he said after a moment, the scent of her perfume drifting around him like a cloud. "I think Monica and Peter looked very happy."

"I think they are," she sighed, turning to look at the happy couple as they sat side-by-side at the table of honor on the dais, then back up to Lucas. "I think they always will be."

"What about you, Olivia?" He heard himself ask the question and knew it was a dangerous one, but he couldn't seem to stop from asking. "Are you happy?"

"Of course," she said quickly.

"Of course," he repeated, feeling foolish now for having asked. "What am I thinking? You're going to have a baby. That's a happy time in a woman's life."

He felt something, he just didn't know what it was—not until her body went rigid, not until her eyes filled with tears and she came to an abrupt halt.

"Oh, my God, the baby," she gasped, her hands moving to her abdomen. "The baby."

"What?" he demanded, not understanding. "Olivia, what is it? Are you all right?"

She was nodding as she looked up at him, a tear brimming over her lashes and spilling onto her cheek. "The baby moved. I felt the baby move."

Even though the music continued to play and couples sailed past them on the dance floor, it was as if nothing else existed. He covered her hands with his, looked into her eyes and felt a little like crying too.

"I know I don't have a right, I know it should be the real father here with you now, but I'm very happy to be the one to share this with you."

"Oh, Lucas," she said after a moment, her bottom lip quivering. "Lucas, I have to tell you something."

Olivia watched the tip of the mountain disappear beneath the clouds, the plane climbing higher as it hurled through the sky, carrying her away from all the pretense and half-truths and back to the cold, hard reality that was her life. The playacting ended here, the charade was over and there would be no more lies. What had started out as a noble effort in hopes of making things better for the people she loved had become an albatross—a millstone that had grown heavier and more weighty with each passing day.

Saying goodbye to her family had been difficult, but she'd been ready to leave. She was anxious to get back to Seattle, anxious to get on with the story, on with the divorce she would concoct so that she could put it behind her and be done with it.

She thought of the wedding, of how happy Monica and Peter had looked and how wonderful it had been to witness them joining their lives in love and in marriage. That was what marriage was meant to be—an open, honest and *real* commitment to love and to honor another—not the farce she'd been playing out for the last seven days. She felt ashamed of herself, sickened by the hoax she'd affected and vowed to repent.

Maybe it was that vow that had made her do what she'd done last night, that had found her looking up into Lucas's eyes and telling him everything. Before she'd had a chance to think, before she'd had a chance to consider motives or weigh options, the truth had come spilling out. Like a purging that cleansed and healed, she had told him about Rachel and Ted, about the favor they had asked and about the accident that had taken their lives and changed hers forever.

Glancing away from the window, she slipped a hand over her abdomen, remembering the tiny fluttering that had brought them both to an abrupt stop on the dance floor. How many times had she heard her patients describe the thrill, the utter exhilaration of feeling their babies move for the first time—hundreds, thousands? Yet even with that, she hadn't been prepared. There was a life inside her, a life that nurtured and protected. What a miracle that was, what a gift.

She thought of how Lucas had covered her hands with his, how he had looked when he realized what had just happened. She wished Rachel and Ted could have been there to share in that moment, but since it couldn't be them, she was glad it was Lucas who had shared that special moment with her. She had seen the emotion in his face, had appreciated his reaction just as she'd come to appreciate so much he had done in the last seven days. Something had snapped in her brain, some realization or resolution that prevented her from continuing the sham.

After everything she'd put him through this last week, she owed him the truth.

"Will this bother you?"

Olivia turned, looking up at the small reading light Lucas pointed to above their seats. "No, that's fine."

He reached up and switched on the light, adjusting it to shine directly on to his newspaper. He'd barely said ten words to her since they'd gotten up this morning, not that there'd been much time for conversation. Their flight out of Santa Barbara had been early, giving them just enough time to finish packing and make their hasty goodbyes, but she could already see that things had changed between them. His job was over, it was no longer necessary for him to behave as her husband so it was now time for them to go back to being...

She shifted against the seat, glancing back out the small window of the plane again. What did they go back to being? They may not be man and wife, but they were hardly strangers any longer. And while a part of her was sick of the playacting and the lies, she had to admit she had enjoyed being someone special to him, even if it had been just an illusion, just part of the job he was doing. Marriage and a family had been a sweet fantasy and she had to admit she felt a little letdown at the thought of going back to being just another person to him, someone not very special and not particularly important in his life. Still, she would have thought that resuming their real lives would have eased the tension between them, but instead it seemed to have made things worse. Of course, some of the awkwardness could be because she had told him the truth about the baby, but she suspected it had more to do with what happened after that.

There was a lot she didn't know about Lucas McCall, but she knew him well enough to know he was a good, kind, compassionate man who wouldn't stand in judgment of her. Still his reaction to the truth about her child had surprised her. As she'd expected, he hadn't moralized or criticized, hadn't lectured or censured her. What she hadn't expected was for him to sweep her up into his arms and kiss her so gently, so sweetly, it left her breathless and weak.

Brave. That's what he'd called her. Brave, generous and loving. He said he respected her for the choices she'd made and admired her for her unselfishness. Even now the words reverberated in her brain, making her feel warm and weak. And then there had been that kiss—so different from the one at the rehearsal dinner, but no less powerful.

"It's raining in Seattle."

She turned and glanced down at the page he was reading. "Is it really?"

"Sixteen inches since the start of the month."

"Rain in Seattle," she murmured dryly. "Who would have guessed?"

He glanced up, looking almost surprised at the humor. "Yeah, I guess that's hardly news."

She turned and looked out the window again, blinking back the moisture that rose in her eyes. It had to be hormones making her lose perspective and making her feel like she wanted to burst into tears. Good heavens, what was the matter with her? The way she felt you'd think they really *were* breaking up.

She'd known all along this day would happen, that they would get back to Seattle and go their separate ways. That had been the idea from the beginning. It was just plain dumb to take it personally or to feel let down. After all, it wasn't as though anything that had happened between them had been real, it had all been an act, just part of the charade. No doubt it was her delicate condition causing her to get caught up in the fantasy, her screwy hormones making this more difficult than it should be, making her feel badly about the end of a marriage—even a phony one. And it wasn't like she wasn't ever going to see him again. They could still be friends. They had been before, there was no reason for that not to continue. But to think that there could be anything else—well, that was silly. He was Lucas McCall for heaven's sake. He no doubt could have any woman he wanted. Why in the world would he want to get involved with a woman who was going to have a baby?

"Would either of you care for some coffee?"

They turned in unison to the flight attendant in the aisle.

"Nothing for me, thanks," she said, shaking her head, hoping her eyes didn't look as watery as they felt.

He shook his head, waving the attendant past, then turned to her. "You feeling okay?"

"Fine, why?" She hoped that hadn't sounded as defensive to him as it had to her.

"I just know the mornings haven't been the best times for you lately."

A picture of him sitting on the rim of the bathtub while she sat on the floor with her head over the toilet flashed in her brain and she groaned. "Maybe not, but I think I'm getting beyond that."

He looked at her for a moment, then nodded. "Good."

There was another incredibly long, awkward moment. Finally, he picked up his newspaper and went back to reading, which only made her feel like crying even more.

"Hormones," she whispered, leaning back into the seat and closing her eyes. "Screwy, screwy hormones."

"You say something?"

Her lids sprang open and she turned to him. "Just talking to myself."

He nodded again and went back to his paper. The landing in San Francisco was smooth. Gratefully the layover was brief and rushed, and the packed flight to Seattle distracting enough to make the time pass quickly. Otherwise, Olivia wasn't sure she would have been able to stand it. Now that it was over she wanted it over, she wanted him to walk out of her life and get it over with so she didn't have to think about it any longer. She'd be fine once she got back to her apartment and back to work. It wouldn't matter then if he looked at her with cold, unfeeling eyes, it wouldn't matter that she meant nothing to him. She'd get used to it. She had the baby and that was all she needed.

And then there it was—the finale, the finish, the

end—the spot where they parted company. Suddenly she was waiting at the cabstand at the airport in Seattle—rain pouring down, wind blowing. She would take one taxi, he another.

"This is for you," she said, handing him a check from her personal account. "With my thanks."

Lucas looked down at the paper in his hands. "I don't want this."

"Why not? You earned it." If she hadn't known better, she would have thought it was anger she saw in his eyes when he'd looked at her. "I want you to take it."

"Olivia, I don't need the money."

"Maybe not. But it's what we agreed on. And I owe you so much more." She extended her hand, hoping she could get into the cab before the tears started to fall. "Goodbye, Lucas."

"You owe me nothing," he said in a tight voice as he turned and stalked towards the other waiting cab. But after a few steps he stopped, spinning around and rushing back. "Except this."

With that, he dragged her into his arms, stealing her breath with a kiss that was as brutal as it was passionate. He spared nothing, ravishing her lips despite the rain, despite the crowd and despite her delicate condition. It was a hungry kiss, tinged with anger and regret, one that spoke of need and desire and so much that had been left unsaid. Olivia forgot about where she was, forgot even who she was. Her world consisted only of this man, and the emotion that squeezed at her heart.

"That one, Dr. Martin," he growled, setting her away from him, "was on the house."

Chapter Ten

"That's it, the last one."

Olivia looked up from the chart she was reviewing, peering over the top of her glasses to the young woman standing at the door. Diane Mathers had worked as her office manager since she'd started her practice and Olivia had no doubt the place would fold if not for Diane's efficient and expert handling. "Why don't you knock off early, Diane? It's nearly four—no sense you hanging around here."

"You mean it?" Diane asked skeptically, sliding the file drawer closed. "You sure you won't be needing me for anything else? I could start on those case studies—"

"Get out of here," Olivia insisted, cutting her off and waving her back. Diane didn't know about the baby yet, but Olivia knew that when she did, there would be no embarrassing questions, no tasteless remarks. "Go spend a little time with that darling son of yours."

The young woman smiled. "Really? You wouldn't mind?"

"Get out."

"You won't forget to lock the file drawer, will you?" she asked, backing towards the door.

"Get out."

"And you know how to log off the computer, don't you?"

"Get out."

"And you'll remember to set the night bell on your private line?"

"Get out or you're fired."

Diane beamed. "Thanks, Olivia. Good night."

Olivia smiled as she watched the young woman disappear around the corner. It had been almost a week since the wedding—six long, grueling, exhausting days that hadn't been busy enough to stop her from thinking about Lucas. It was ridiculous, it made no sense, but she missed him. What was the matter with her? Had she lost her mind?

She glanced down at the chart in front of her, tapping the point of her pen against the edge. She really hadn't expected him to be on the night shift at the clinic but it had been a disappointment to see Gus patrolling the halls again. Besides, he'd explained to her that it was just something he did from time to time, something to keep him in touch with his clients and his employees. Still, it would have been the perfect excuse if he had wanted to see her again, to check in on her and see how she was doing, but it was obvious he wasn't interested. And why should he be. He'd done her a favor and that was the end of it. Why couldn't she just put it all behind her and get on with things?

"Working hard?"

Olivia looked up at Monica and Peter standing in the doorway of her office and slowly lowered the chart to her desk. "W-what are you two doing here?"

"You can't stay on a honeymoon forever," Monica said, starting across the room. "We had a layover on the flight back from Honolulu and thought we'd talk you and Lucas into an early dinner."

"I can't believe it," Olivia said as she stood up and rounded the desk. She met her sister halfway, hugging her tight. "I—I'm stunned. How are you? How was the honeymoon?"

"How are you?" Monica asked, her voice serious now.

"Me? I'm fine. Never felt better."

"Well you look positively glowing," Peter said, stepping into the office. "I hope it's all right, just popping in like this. There was no one at the desk outside."

"All right?" Olivia said, hugging him too. "Of course it's all right. I'm thrilled. As a matter of fact, I was thinking of going home a little early today."

"Okay then," Monica said. "Give that hubby of yours a call and let's bust out of here. Last ones married have to pay."

Olivia's smile fell despite Monica's joking. "Oh, uh, Lucas...he's been really busy."

"Then he needs a break," Monica said, walking

past Olivia to her desk and picking up the phone. "What's his number, I'll give him a call."

"Oh, no." Olivia shook her head, rushing to the desk and taking the phone from her sister. "I really don't think he'll be able to get away. He's had so much going on since we got back."

"Well, why don't we give him a call and just ask anyway," Monica suggested. "Besides, I'd at least like to say hello to him."

"And I'd like to, too," Peter added.

Olivia stood there holding the phone in her hand as though she were ready to beat them off with it. What did she do now?

"Well, I, uh, I suppose we could try and call," she stammered, thinking there had to be a listing for McCall Security in the phone book.

"Would it be better if we just stopped by his office?" Monica suggested. "Maybe surprise him too?"

"No, I'll call," Olivia insisted, shaking her head. "I'll...I'll call. I'll..." She rounded the desk again and pulled out a drawer wondering how she would explain having to look his number up in the book. "I'll...call." Only, as she moved to reach for the telephone directory inside the drawer, something outside in the corridor caught her attention. As she straightened up, the telephone slipped from her hand, falling onto her desk with a loud clank. "My God, Lucas, you're here."

Lucas brought the car to a stop in the parking lot, wondering what the hell he was doing. Reaching into his pocket, he pulled out the check, staring down at Olivia's scrawled doctor's signature. It had been his intention to hand it back to her, to put it into her hands and tell her he didn't expect payment for helping out a friend—and they were friends! At least he was determined they stay friends. He had no idea what she thought about it.

He folded the check and put it back in his pocket, remembering how furious he'd been when she'd handed it to him. Talk about seeing red! Somehow he'd thought they'd gotten beyond their business arrangement during the course of the week, that they'd shifted from their former employer-employee status and moved on to something like a friendship, but obviously she hadn't felt the same way.

He kicked open the car door, stepping out on to the pavement and making it across the wet parking lot with long, determined strides. Well, he'd decided he was going to do whatever it took to change her mind. He had hoped getting back to his old routine would help him get her out of his system, help him put things into perspective and back on track. All it succeeded in doing, however, was to show him just how important she had become to him. He hadn't been able to stop thinking of her, couldn't stop worrying about her and caring about how she and the baby were doing.

He'd never known anyone like her, anyone so generous and so caring. First she had agreed to bear the child her friends couldn't have, and then she'd assumed the responsibility of raising that child when her friends had died. Not many women would have agreed to such an undertaking, certainly not any of the women he had known.

He understood things now—the reason she'd told her family about getting married, her need for an instant husband. It took a lot of guts to put her own feelings aside for the greater good of those she loved, to care enough that everyone felt comfortable with the situation, and he admired that. She may not need a real husband and she may be perfectly capable of taking care of herself and her child without any help from anyone, but he couldn't seem to stop himself from wanting to reach out. He wasn't interested in being the white knight, didn't want to ride to the rescue. He just wanted her in his life. He'd gone off the deep end for her, went *way* out on a limb, but he'd come to care about her whether she liked it or not and he wanted a place in her life, even if it was just as her friend. He couldn't make her feel something that she didn't, but they had shared something special, something he didn't want to lose. He'd had to fight for everything in his life and he was prepared to fight for her too.

The corridor leading to her office was practically deserted and the leather soles of his loafers sounded loud and out of place against the linoleum floor. He was nervous, something he didn't think he'd felt since he sat on that airplane in Santa Barbara waiting to meet his new in-laws. It was the end of the workday at the close of a long, hard week—he had no idea what kind of greeting he would get from her, whether she'd be pleased, surprised, or annoyed.

He could hear voices coming from the open doorway leading to her office and he came to an abrupt halt. He'd come this far, he wasn't about to be deterred. Still, if he was going to throw himself at her mercy, he really would rather not have an audience. Leaning back against the wall where he'd once stood and listened to her talking to that escort service, he prepared himself to wait it out—until he heard his name mentioned. Pushing himself away from the wall, he stepped around the corner. And while he may not have known what kind of greeting to expect, he certainly didn't expect the one he got.

"Lucas, you're here, what a surprise," she said, rushing around the desk and into his arms.

The look on her face had his pulse tripping into overtime and for a moment, he thought maybe she had missed him as much as he'd missed her. She looked even more beautiful, more radiant than he'd remembered and he thought his heart was going to burst. It was only after she'd pressed her lips to his ear and whispered *"Please"* that he noticed Monica and Peter standing behind her and understood what she was asking.

"Here I came to surprise you," he said, falling into the role of husband again. "And I'm the one surprised." Giving her a wink, he set her away and turned to Monica and Peter. "Don't tell me you decided to trade all that Hawaiian sun for a little Seattle rain?"

"Just long enough for a layover," Monica said, giving him a hug and a kiss. "And to take my favorite sister and her husband out for an early dinner."

"How does that sound?" Peter asked, shaking Lucas's outstretched hand.

"Sounds great, except for one thing."

Monica's smile stiffened. "What's that?"

He turned to Olivia, slipping a hand around her waist and pulling her close. "This is our town. *We're* taking you out."

Olivia watched as they passed beneath the freeway sign, trying to prepare herself for the inevitable. Just a few more blocks and they would be back at the clinic, having come full circle. Monica and Peter were on their way back to Santa Barbara and she'd managed to dodge the bullet one more time. They'd come and gone and were none the wiser.

Dinner had been surprisingly pleasant. Monica and Peter had been exuberant from their honeymoon vacation in Hawaii and had entertained them with stories of their adventures and discoveries. Lucas had been charming and friendly, and she'd had a hard time taking her eyes off him. It was a little unnerving just how easily they had slipped back into their roles as a married couple again, unnerving to realize how much she had missed being his wife.

Lucas turned the steering wheel, slipping his plush European luxury car into the stall next to her aging car.

"I'll follow you home," he said, taking the car out of gear and turning off the ignition.

She turned and looked at him, the glow from the streetlight streaking across his face in the darkness. "I appreciate it, but that's not necessary. I've imposed on you enough for one evening." She shook her head, dropping her gaze to her hands as they twisted the handle of her purse. "Lucas, I...I don't know what to say. I can't even begin to thank you.

I saw Monica and Peter at the door and I just panicked.'' She looked up. ''I'm not sure what I would have done if you hadn't come along just then.''

''Sounds like my timing was pretty good then.''

''Good, I'd call it more like miraculous,'' she said with a small laugh. ''I never did ask why you came by. Did you need to see me for something?''

''Actually there was some business I needed to take care of.''

Her smile fell. ''Business.''

''Right, some loose ends I needed to tie up.''

''I see.'' She undid her seat belt and reached for the door handle, feeling foolish and embarrassed. She thought he'd come to see her, thought maybe he'd missed her and was coming by to say hello. ''Well, it was fortunate for me. I won't keep you any longer,'' she said with a small laugh in an effort to hide her discomfort. ''Thank you again and hopefully I won't have to call on you again to play the part of my husband.''

''Is that a promise?''

She blinked, surprised, and felt heat climb up her neck. There had been nothing teasing in his voice, nothing humorous or funny. He was serious. ''Uh, absolutely.''

''Olivia, I'm afraid I'm going to need a little something more than that.''

She stopped as she reached for the door. ''What?''

''I'm afraid I'm going to need something more than your promise that you won't ask me to pretend to be your husband again?''

''Something more?'' She shook her head, feeling

a little as though she'd taken an arrow right in the heart. "Look, Lucas, I said I was sorry I imposed on you this evening and I promise it won't happen again." She pushed open the car door. "You want me to sign something?"

"No, I want you to marry me."

Olivia let the door swing shut, her entire body going numb. She couldn't have heard him right. How could he have just asked her to marry him? He didn't want to portray her husband. There had to be some kind of mistake.

"Y-you...what?" she stammered.

"The way I see it, the practice run went so good, we might as well try it for real."

She could barely hear for the ringing in her ears. "Lucas, you can't be serious."

"And it's not like I'm asking you to feel something you don't. You need someone, you and the baby. I want to help you, to be there for you and maybe in time..." He paused, shaking his head. "Who knows, feelings can grow."

"You want to marry me so you can help?"

He leaned across the seat, pulling her close. "Olivia, I want to marry you because I love you. I don't want to play games anymore, I don't want to playact or pretend." He ran a hand along her cheek, cupping her chin. "I don't want to be a make-believe husband. I want to be a real husband—your husband." Bringing her lips to his, he kissed her long and deep. "Olivia, I love you. Marry me. Make me the happiest man in the world."

"But, Lucas, the baby—"

"I love that little baby inside you—it's part of

you and I want it to be a part of me too. I don't want to lose either one of you.'' He brushed his lips against hers. ''Tell me you love me, Olivia. Tell me you'll be my wife—for real this time.''

Olivia felt the tears pouring down her cheeks, blurring her vision and spilling down on to her dress, but she didn't care. Lucas loved her, he wanted to marry her and that was all that mattered.

''Are…are you sure?''

''I'm sure.''

''For real this time?''

He kissed her again—long and deep. ''Absolutely for real.''

''Oh, Lucas, I do love you.''

''Then prove it. Marry me.''

''I will, Lucas—for real this time.''

* * * * * *

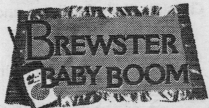

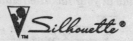

**Start celebrating Silhouette's 20th anniversary
with these 4 special titles by
New York Times bestselling authors**

Fire and Rain*
by Elizabeth Lowell

King of the Castle
by Heather Graham Pozzessere

State Secrets*
by Linda Lael Miller

Paint Me Rainbows*
by Fern Michaels

On sale in December 1999

Plus, a special free book offer inside each title!

Available at your favorite retail outlet

*Also available on audio from Brilliance.

Silhouette®
Where love comes alive™

Visit us at www.romance.net   PSNYT_R